THE INDIAN EMERGENCY

THE INDIAN EMERGENCY

Kumar Kinshuk

NU VOICE
PRESS

NU VOICE
PRESS

First published by NU VOICE PRESS 2024
An imprint of Hubhawks Pvt. Ltd
www.nuvoicepress.com

This is a work of fiction. Space and time have been rearranged to suit the convenience of the book. Except for public figures, hotels, and institution names, any resemblance to persons living or dead or the real events are purely coincidental. The opinions expressed in the book are those of the characters, and should not be confused with that of the Author.

ISBN: 978-81-966888-8-2

Typeset by Saanvi Graphics, Noida
Printed at Thomson Press
Published by Nu Voice Press

DISCLAIMER

As the author is in the process of learning Urdu, the translations used in the book aim to convey the essence while respecting the language's nuances. Readers are encouraged to consider the story's context and not regard them as strictly literal translations.

I would like to dedicate this book to the victims of the Indian Emergency.

Author's Note 2024

I wrote this novel during the Covid-19 Lockdown Unlock 4.0 period. It was started on the 10th of October, 2020 and completed on the 26th of October, 2020. The research for the book took over two years, wherein I conducted multiple interviews with people who had seen the Emergency unfold in their lives, and later experienced the joys of freedom, once again.

Come to think about it. For the people of a newly-founded Republic, who had struggled for hundreds of years to regain its place under the sun, seeing a multitude of state actions unfolding in front of them—the imposition of MISA (Maintenance of Internal Security Act, 1971), extreme power in the hands of the police, the incarceration of journalists and common people alike and without trials, and a continuous price hike in goods and commodities of daily use, was deeply unsettling, as they saw their fledgling democratic state allegedly turn into an authoritarian one. There were mass protests and a government crackdown against the Press. Human rights were suspended unconditionally. The governance was almost tyrannical, and a dystopian view gained ground amongst the masses. The Police had unbridled powers. Laws were in a state of suspended animation. The idea of a democratic India was dying a slow and poisonous death. The worst fears of our freedom fighters had come true for the nation.

Those were tough times. Lok Nayak Jai Prakash Narain called for a total revolution against the way the nation was being governed. Only one party had ruled the country ever since the independence, and one family had held on to the reigns for far too long. During my interviews with the people, I found them emotional and with horror writ large over their faces, as they spoke about those times. It was the worst type of crisis the country was facing, both politically and economically. The people felt that there was a chance the country would have fallen to anarchy, and gone the route our neighbouring country had. It had to be brought back from the brink of a disaster, one with monumental proportions.

While I explore the era and the political landscape of the Emergency in this book, my effort is to share stories of love and passion, of friendship, and of perseverance and devotion. This is a social book with a political backdrop, a rather surcharged one. One of my protagonists in the novel is a *Shayar*. So, I had to devote some time to learn the basics of Urdu, which is one of the finest languages when it comes to portraying one's deepest thoughts and emotions. Let me tell you, while it was quite an effort to learn a new language—I was focused, as I had to write beautiful Urdu poems and couplets to express the protagonist's deepest feelings in this novel. It took me a while to construct this poignant story. While plotting the basic construct of the story, I let my heart bleed blue.

I genuinely hope this book touches your heart.

Character List

Dhiraj Sahay – A Professor.

Nilima Sahay – Dhiraj's wife and homemaker.

Niru – Dhiraj's daughter.

Appu – Dhiraj's son.

Dr. A. N. Sahay – Dhiraj's father.

Ahindra Pandit – A Jailer.

Anjana Pandit – Ahindra's wife.

Deepak Pandit – Ahindra's elder son.

Kul Pandit – Ahindra's younger son.

Umar Farooqui – A Shayar.

Begum Najma Farooqui – Umar's wife.

Rajendra Agarwal – A Businessman.

Chitra Agarwal – Rajendra's wife and homemaker.

Guria Agarwal – Rajendra's daughter.

Amit Agarwal – Rajendra's son.

Sameer Agarwal – Deceased elder brother of Rajendra.

Nakul Mandal – Amit's classmate.

Tarachand Kajaria – A Businessman.

Maulana Saheb – A religious leader in Patna.

Nakul Bose – A Police Inspector in Patna.

Chapter 1
1973

"Deepak, why is it so difficult? Why are you so afraid of love marriage? Let me tell *Babu* to meet *Panditji*. They would sort it out. After all, this is the twentieth century!"

"Guria, you know I am going to speak to my father on this. Why are you so worried?" Deepak asked.

"Because I cannot see my life without you. Why are you so timid?"

"I too cannot see myself without you, Guria. I really hope our destinies are intertwined. We are great together and we will have a good life," Deepak spoke thoughtfully.

Guria was in a rueful mood. They were perched on the steps of a temple in the Kadamkuan area of Patna. It was dusk and the two had planned to meet at the temple. Guria wished to implore Deepak to get his parents to agree to their marriage.

Bells tolled a couple of times breaking their monotony. Both were in deep thought. They mulled over all their options, considering for a moment to marry at the temple itself, the very next day. They could easily elope and start their dream life, however their faith in the institution of marriage refrained them to do so. In Indian society, since ages ago, marriages have worked if the bride and groom have been blessed by the elders. As they say in India—the marriage is not just between two people but also between two families. And, who doesn't love a grand ceremony?

One could inhale a mixture of marigold, chrysanthemums, and roses decaying in the air. The aroma must have been from the flowers in front of the deities. People hurried to their destinations, on rickshaws, cycles, and scooters. Some people were tired after the day's work, some looked hopeful for a good dinner at home, while some looked downright bored and dejected. They were possibly working in jobs they loathed and life itself was a daily burden for them.

Deepak broke the quiet around them and said, "I have not been able to speak to my dad. He is a firm believer of the caste system that's been propagated by the priests for centuries."

"I know. I have heard this for the umpteenth time and believe me, it is not music to my ears. I enjoy the quiet here more than your words. What have we finally come to?"

Deepak felt a bit shaken because of Guria's sudden outburst.

"I was planning to tell dad about you a few days back, but he came home after what was seemingly a bad day. He had gone to attend a marriage ceremony where, according to him, the bride was from an upper caste and the groom from a lower caste."

He adjusted his glasses on his nose, and continued, "See, frankly speaking, I do not understand the Hindu caste system. However, I saw Panditji pained at the way he thought our society was sinking. According to him, *Kalyug* was truly here. He seemed anxious, out of breath, and morose. He kept on saying that people have forgotten their *dharma* and their *karma*. Adding that such marriages were not blessed by the Gods, and that such marriages would turn families and entire generations into an uncultured and uncouth bunch."

"Enough of it, Deepak! I heard you. I know you cannot do much as you truly love your dad and your family. I would also not advise you to elope with me as that isn't something I would like to do myself," Guria said, getting up and patting her back for any dust on her salwar. She wore a deep yellow *churidar* and *kurta*, embroidered at its hem. Simple but elegant.

Deepak took the cue and got up. He patted his jeans, gave some air to his shirt that felt a bit crumpled near his belly, folded the sleeves upwards, and gazed lovingly and longingly at Guria. He knew another day was getting over soon and he had not even spoken to his mom yet, let alone his dad. He knew he had to find the courage to speak to his family about the mess he was in. He was deeply in love with Guria, and had not been able to confess it even to his brother, Kul, who was younger than Deepak only by a couple of years. Kul had suspected that his brother was in love, but he also knew Deepak better than Deepak himself. He knew it would be of no use to goad Deepak into accepting something if he did not want to speak about it. Kul knew Deepak would take his own sweet time to get out of his mess, and so he left him to himself.

Deepak suddenly blurted, half believing what he said, "I think he will never allow us to get married. We would have to look at other options eventually, like going to the marriage registrar and getting married; or better still, we might have to elope, which of course, neither of us wish to do."

"I am game! I would not like it, though. My parents would bless us either way. I have already spoken to them. They will do whatever it takes to get us married," saying this, Guria waved her hands to remove a fly perched on her nose, but it came back, moving around Guria. Guria flicked at it, thoughtfully saying, "But you must take your own call."

"Hmmm..."

"Anyway, by when are you going to begin your new job? Haven't they asked you to join by the 1st of the coming month? It's in Delhi, right?" Guria asked.

Deepak saw the fly again on Guria's hair, and with a quick movement of his right palm, caught it. He kept the fly in his palm for a moment too long and then released it away from Guria. Guria had a sparkle in her eyes but kept her praise for Deepak's reflexes to herself, for the moment. She knew they were in an important discussion, and she could not disturb it. Deepak read her thoughts, as he always did so well, and said,

"Yes darling, this fly almost single-handedly took us away from our agenda for the day. Forget it, we must continue our subject."

"Deepak, our agenda has always been the love we feel for each other. It can never be a discussion about our marriage. I don't know, but I have felt bugged over the past few days, and wished to speak to you regarding your plans."

She nervously adjusted her hair, pushing a strand behind her right ear. Deepak slowly caressed her forehead, gently took his finger towards her neck and then back towards her ear, getting the strand out from her ear's grasp, back on her face. He loved her hair and wanted to caress it whenever possible. He liked her as she was, carefully careless. Guria had a smile on her lips and looked at Deepak with love. Deepak knew that her pouting face, with locks of her hair on the two sides, was jostling for its space on her glowing face. She was indeed ravishing, and at dusk, under the golden light of the sun, she looked charming and ethereal.

Deepak said, "Before I just die staring at you, after sucking every essence from your body, which I intend to do, let us complete our discussion."

Guria flushed. "Okay Deepak, let us conclude for the day."

"My dad has always wanted me to join the police force to carry on the family tradition, but I will go ahead with my decision to go for a normal job." He twitched his facial muscles a bit and said, "I cannot see myself as a policeman. I am an outlier of sorts. Kul could possibly join the police. Does he not have the build to boot?"

"Oh, so am I madly in love with the wrong guy? Should I not have been with Kul, who has a better physique and who could be in the forces? Just the thought of it is so exciting!"

"You are definitely having a field day throwing all this muck at me. Enough, give me a kiss now. Come on!"

"What on earth, Deepak! We are in the precinct of a temple in front of so many people and you want a kiss from me?" Guria winked, making an adorable pout.

"After the amount of mud that you threw at me, it is only right to give me a kiss. Okay, come on, at least kiss me on my cheeks."

Their playful banter continued as they heralded an auto rickshaw. Both got in. Deepak would drop Guria near her house, before going back to his own.

They went back to their homes, happy with their plan. Guria wanted Deepak to eventually join her father's business. He was a trader of various agricultural goods and was at the top of his trade. He was doing very well, and he could do with two more hands to grow his business further.

Guria knew that Deepak was a contrarian and would probably not have those archaic thoughts about not working for his father-in-law. However, she wanted to integrate him into the family business rather carefully. She wanted it to happen as a gradual decision and not as a careful strategy. Else, it could hurt his male ego.

Guria knew she could convince her dad and get Deepak a job in his firm. It would be an easy thing for her. She had to be careful though, with Deepak. She had to time it well, so that he would agree to join his father-in-law's business eventually. Whilst she was making all the plans with Deepak as the protagonist of her story, seldom did she know, 'Man proposes, and God disposes!'

Chapter 2

1975

"Send the next prisoner in!" Ahindra Pandit, the prison jailor in Patna commanded. He was a short and stout man, sporting a clean-shaven face with a bold and heavy moustache. He had a round face, was forty-eight years old, but had sharp features and quirky mannerisms. He was fidgety, and he could not stay still for long. He would move his arms and legs, get up from his seat, sit down, exercise his limbs and his big eyes at sudden intervals. His nose might not put Pinocchio to shame, but it had its own presence on his face. He was well combed with whatever was left to comb, well-bred, and well-mannered. He was quite unlike the normal policeman of yore in the state of Bihar. He used euphemisms when necessary and his language was parliamentary.

An erudite person walked in with a calm expression, unusual for seeing prisoners getting into prison for the first time. He was of an average Indian height, was dark complexioned, and his gait was that of a confident and well-read person. Ahindra seemed transfixed with this prisoner who had just walked in. Dhiraj Sahay was a Professor of English Literature at the Simdega College.

"Namaste Jailor *saheb*, if I may call you thus!" The Professor nodded in respect for the jailor.

Pat came the reply, "Namaste Professor saheb. Please call me Panditji." His name was Ahindra Pandit. But since he was a *Brahmin* by caste, people called him Panditji. Panditji, the word was used with reverence for a person from the upper caste, who was well versed in the Vedas, and who considered the service to God as his karma. Jailor Ahindra Pandit liked himself to be known as Panditji.

"Panditji it will be. Hope you are doing good."

"Surprised to see men of honour making it a regular practice to come to our prison. We have been used to welcoming thugs and murderers but having respectable people like you... gives me jitters."

"Panditji, I don't know what honour is left in this country. We seemingly gave birth to a country in 1947, which was a democracy. There was supposed to be, amongst other things, human rights. But what have we been reduced to as a nation today?"

"We are a nation of great men, and we tower over many other nation states, Professor saheb."

"So be it. I do not wish to debate while I am entering a prison as a prisoner."

"I welcome you to the jail precincts, professor saheb. My people will show you to your barrack and they will guide you so that you can easily mix in the crowd," the jailor said, adjusting his thick glasses on his nose. He then got up, stretched his hands outwards and sat back in his seat before saying, "I have asked them to give you an easy spot, not mixed with murderers and hardcore criminals, but in between some petty thugs and other political prisoners. Since you have been held under MISA (Maintenance of Internal Security Act), your human rights have been suspended and you don't have anything real to count on. So, don't engage in political debates and arguments, and keep away from motley crowds with an agenda."

"Absolutely clear on the directions, Panditji." The Professor nodded and moved outwards from the jailor's chamber.

He was taken to his barracks. Dhiraj had seen jail barracks only in movies up till then. This was nothing like the nice prisons he had seen in Hindi movies earlier. This was different. He felt nauseous. His heart bled a thousand cuts against the oppression meted out to fellow humans. He was a creative person, and he felt a deep and unrelenting pain in his mind. He knew that this was the way of showing his resolve to fight the injustice in the country. They had a democratically elected government which was hell bent on quashing the freedom of its people.

What he then saw was a picture of complete disarray. There were a few people who looked like they were possibly political prisoners, detained under the MISA, while others were obviously crooks. He went in rather slowly but with firm steps, looked at people, while others looked at him in wonder.

"Look! Another fool has come today!"

"Oh, they think they can change the country through their will power and their protests."

"This government is strong, and they know how to quell this movement. He will not survive a day here!"

"What do you smell here, brother? Pee, or latrine? Or our dirty skin? Or our breath? Will you survive tonight?"

Various voices were heard, and the Professor kept quiet, taking it all in. He looked at the people around without any hatred, but with a softness on his face and pain in his eyes. He knew the country was poor and a multitude of Indians lived under the poverty line. He could see thugs and crooks who were from the lowest strata of the society and must have taken to theft for keeping themselves afloat. The country and the governments had to keep their promise to the nation. It was a time for nation-building, which successive governments ever since independence were focused on, but that was not enough. He knew what the country was reduced to at the hour was merely a combination of forces hell-bent on keeping the governance in their hands, by hook or crook. The Professor quickly noted that some of the crooks might hurt him if he did not do something fast. He knew it was a given to protect their territory. The Professor would soon be assigned to the biggest crook, and would be expected to work under his orders. That was not to be.

He said in a booming voice, a voice that was deep and sonorous, "I respect your souls, one and all. I am a teacher and have met the biggest of criminals in the past, who despite my young age, have always touched my feet. I will help you heal and see the light you couldn't see in this life of yours. I am happy all of you are associated with passionate souls who care for the freedom of this nation and its people. Let us be the guiding light and let us pull ourselves up to give our Mother Earth, the freedom that she deserves."

As he said this, silence filled the barrack containing almost forty people. The Professor could see two men walking up towards him. One was tall and had a burly tummy, long-ish face, serious demeanour, but an overall positive look. He had a lighter complexion.

The other person was of an average height with a stubble and a moustache. He wore a skull cap and walked upright with honour, and looked distinguished. He seemed like a man of knowledge and creativity.

The taller person said that he was Rajendra Agarwal, a businessman, also serving sentence under the MISA, but he was a fighter against the tyranny of the governmental forces and police excesses. The Professor acknowledged Rajendra, shook his hand and quickly moved forward to hug the other person who walked towards him. Rajendra and the other inmates looked at them with inquisitiveness. The other person was a *Shayar*, or simply a poet, and he knew the Professor well. The Professor considered Umar Farooqui or the Shayar as his mentor. The Shayar was also being held under the MISA, but he wished to eradicate this nauseating feeling of being governed in a democracy by oppression. The Professor felt elated.

The barrack understood that a meeting of minds had happened and something good was in store for them. They were constantly stressed due to the constant threats by the guards. They knew these gentlemen would take it back with the guards and fight the oppression and the inhumane living conditions. It wasn't long before a couple of guards came to take a prisoner away for some work. The guy was in mortal fear. He knew he would be thrashed, and some fresh charge would be imposed if he did not comply. There might have been some history. However, he suddenly came running to the Professor and sought his help. The Professor knew that the three of them, that is Rajendra, the Shayar, and himself, had to fight back the jailor. Else, they would be under a constant threat.

The Professor told the angry guards to go away. However, one of them commanded back, "Shut up and stay away from trouble. You are obstructing the police in their duty. Wait and watch, action will be taken against you."

The Professor calmly replied, “Go to the jailor and come back with a plan to act against me. Then we’ll talk.”

Rajendra and the Shayar saw the quiet resolve in the Professor. They knew they were in the company of an upright and honest man who could not be cowed down by threats or undue force. They realised that in the Professor, they had someone who would not only be a friend for life, but also be someone who would guide them in the hours of crisis.

Chapter 3
1973

"Panditji, I wish to speak to you about an important matter. Can we have a conversation now?" Deepak asked his father, Ahindra Pandit.

They were sitting at the dining table, waiting for Deepak's mother, Anjana, to serve them. Anjana was a beautiful lady who had been married off early in her life, at the mere age of twenty. She came from a rich Brahmin family and her father was a priest in one of the most important temples of Dhanbad. He presided over multiple functions and *pujas*, thereby earning a fortune. He was very good at palmistry, and with the money he earned from conducting pujas and reading palms, he had built a four-storeyed house in the heart of the city. He was also close to some of the biggest politicians and civil servants in the area.

Anjana was well versed in the Hindu mythology, and she was habituated to a daily reading of The Gita. She was good at palmistry too, but had chosen not to make it a profession. She loved wearing *saris*. She would wear the ornate ones for special occasions or functions, and the normal cotton ones for her daily wear. She never wore any other form of dressing, including *salwar kameez*, gowns, or any western clothes. She felt comfortable only in saris, but she had quite a liking for *lehengas*. She had a couple of lehengas, one from her own *sangeet* function, and the others that she had recently picked up to wear on her son's sangeet. She was a simple lady—a good cook and a doting mother of her two young sons.

Kul, Deepak's younger brother, was also waiting at the dining table, dribbling his glass of water. He was quite naughty for a nineteen-year-old boy. He was tall, fair, and handsome; and he had a penchant for speaking his heart out. He could not contain his anger at times, and to an outsider, he seemed uncouth. That was not true, however, and Panditji, Deepak, and Anjana were aware. They knew that he wished to have his own voice, in spite of his young age, but he was also respectful, and he followed decorum. It was easy to annoy him, though.

Deepak himself was almost six feet tall and broad-shouldered. He didn't exercise daily, but jogged instead for about an hour. At the age of twenty-two, with his looks, he had a host of female admirers. He knew that he could get any girl of his liking, but he chose Guria. He was quiet but focused. He was respectful to everyone around him, more so towards the elders. He revered his father and loved his mother. Deepak liked Guria for her good manners, kind nature, and stunning looks. She was, in every way, a great match for Deepak. But the only issue was that they were from different castes. Guria was a *Marwari*, and hence it was difficult for them to get married with the blessings of Panditji.

"Before you guys start your conversation, Deepak, let me tell you an important thing," Anjana said. "You have a huge problem coming up. You should go as far away from the North as possible." Having said that, she took a short break to see the reaction of Deepak and others at the table. They were all attentive, willing to hear her out. Anjana coughed and said, "I mean, do not go towards the northern side of Patna or to any north Indian city for the next two years. Whilst you were asleep this afternoon, I, just out of curiosity, happened to read your palm."

Uncharacteristically annoyed and a bit dazed, Deepak interjected, "What is all this, *ma*?"

Anjana had a calming face, and she said in a composed manner, "I cannot repeat myself enough, this is important. Take it as my order and it will protect you from an impending crisis. Is that clear? Now, what did you wish to talk to Panditji about?"

Deepak was clueless on hearing these words, as the importance of his mother's revelation was not lost on him. He respected her palmistry skills and deep knowledge of the Hindu *granthas*. He knew that when she said something of this kind, she had already done exhaustive homework on it, so it was difficult to argue against her. However, he also knew that his entire life was sadly going to change because of this decision.

He was left with no choice but to ask Anjana, "*Mummy*, are you sure? Why do you say so? What if I were to go to Delhi next week? What would happen? Does it have anything to do with my health?" Anjana saw that Deepak was restless and understood it was due to something important. She knew that it was uncharacteristic of Deepak to get miffed in a conversation, so she got worried.

"Deepak, why are you so bothered? What has changed suddenly?"

"I wished to seek Panditji's consent for taking up a job in Delhi. I must join this MNC on the first of the coming month. It is a job in sales, and they are giving me the role of an Assistant Manager. I would oversee the dealers and distributors in my zone of operation. It is a well-paying job, Mummy. And, I cannot let it go just because it happens to be in Delhi, which is in the north of India," Deepak finally stopped and placed a half-questioning, half-pleading look at his parents.

"Look, Deepak. I do not have much to say right now," Panditji finally spoke, "Firstly, you need to figure it out with your mother. If she gives you some chant or a ring that might work to avert the danger that she has foreseen in your future, then you can come to speak with me about your job. But as of now, I do not wish to comment on it. I had already stated in the past that I would have liked you to join the police force. That you do not wish to do so is known to me, and I do not intend to force you," Panditji said and turned towards his plate to thank the Almighty for the food on it. Once he was done praying, he just started eating as though nothing had happened, and that he would not have to make a choice anytime soon.

"Mummy, please tell me you can do something to make my movement to Delhi possible. I know you can come up with something that could negate whatever dark influence that's hovering over me," Deepak almost pleaded to Anjana. Kul made a grunting noise, and everyone looked at him with a questioning face. He immediately raised his hand to apologise. He knew that this was an important discussion for Deepak's future, and he better be quiet for the moment.

Anjana thought for a moment and then said, "Deepak, you are my son. I cannot knowingly allow you to go and fall into a pit. I see grave danger in your future. Why do you have to go to Delhi anyway?" She was perplexed. She said with a questioning look on her face, "Why can't you ask this company of yours to allow you to operate from Patna? They would need good people here at Patna too, right? If not, then just send them a regret letter. That is all there is to it." She relaxed a bit, shifting her position to take a seat at the table. She took some food on her plate and started eating. Upon seeing the look on Deepak's face, she added, "You would join a large firm managing a trading business here in Patna. You do not need to move out anytime soon."

"I wished to go to Delhi because of this job. It was a decent salary and there were incentives based on sales performance. I would have done well... anyway, let me think of the alternate options," Deepak said and started eating.

While all of them were having their food, Anjana saw Kul laughing rather mischievously and asked, "What is it, Kul? What makes you so happy today?"

"Nothing, mummy. I just thought of something that isn't too important, but it made me smile," Kul said, grinning from ear to ear. "Okay tell me, did you know dad before marrying him?"

"Impossible. I had not even seen Panditji prior to our marriage. Well, to be precise, we had this ritual called *gauna* and were kind of married off while I was only twelve. He was also a kid back then. We got together much later when I was almost twenty. So, while I continued to live with my parents, my future was linked to your dad at that young age. I could obviously have not married anyone else. Therefore, having guy friends was out of the question. I had to behave and be a 'good girl'. I had to learn cooking and other household work along with my studies.

"I saw him properly for the first time as an adult when he came to pick me up. But things are different nowadays. I see girls talking to boys even on the roadside. That was unthinkable in our times. Let me also tell you that you would also marry into the families of our choice. We are your parents, and we know what's best for you. We would guide you to a better future. Do not even think about getting blown off your feet by a skimpily clad young lady. They might speak well and have great mannerisms, but they would not be great life partners," Anjana concluded.

"What are you even saying, mummy? I do not agree with you on this one bit," Kul protested. "Any girl who dresses differently from your sense of dressing and speaks to guys would not make a good wife and a good mother, according to you? Do you really think so? Then let me tell you, the future of our country is down in the dumps, because all marriages in the future would be love marriages," Kul got into his well-known monologues that he resorted to whenever he felt the need to raise his voice for the others to see reason. He continued, while everyone silently listened to him, "I do not see why liberated women are bad for family making. They could, in fact, raise children who are aware of the rights of women and would be more grounded. They would adapt to such situations better, and therefore, create balanced families." Kul adjusted his hands on the table, and waited for a moment to realise that he had the attention from everyone, and said, "What is wrong in women going out to earn a living? Or, in women willing to take on audacious tasks? The world is changing, mummy. Please accept it, and change yourself and Panditji too. The more you adapt to the present changes in the society, the better the future would be." Kul gulped down a glass of water, having made his point and opinion clear to everyone.

Deepak felt a bit uncomfortable at the turn the conversation had taken, but he had to carry on the mantle of being the elder son. He could not dare speak to his parents in that fashion. However, he couldn't agree more with his younger brother. Deepak could sense his father getting a bit upset, but he had already given up on his younger son. He did not expect much from Kul. But he expected a lot from the elder, so Deepak had to protect his reputation.

"I see that Deepak agrees with your thoughts, Kul, but he cannot take a stand in front of us. That is only due to his respect for us. I do not mean to say that you don't respect us, but you are much more direct in your interactions," Panditji said and took off his heavy glasses for effect, kept it in his left hand for a moment, looked at Kul intently and said, "You cannot keep your thoughts to yourself, even out of the considerations of age or respect. If you believe in something, you blurt it out. Your elder brother, however, is different," Panditji continued while others listened with rapt attention—as it was a rule of sorts in the family that if Panditji spoke, one had to listen and agree to whatever he uttered. He was a learned man who mostly kept to himself. He would only speak when provoked, but he would speak with a lot of conviction.

He resumed, having finished the last morsel on his plate, "Kul, you will go far in your life and your career, but only if you know how to take the right stand at the right time. Decisions make or break careers and lives. I implore the both of you to have the strength of character to back your convictions."

He looked at both Deepak and Kul, waited for their reaction, studied it for a millisecond and continued, "We might be from a generation or two before you, and our perspectives might differ from yours, but you need to educate us for your own good. I am impressed by your thoughts and the way you fought for girls and their rights." Panditji beamed, and it showed on his face. He gave a short nod to Anjana, who responded with a smile and a nod.

Panditji continued, "It is profound, and I feel that we have raised a good person. Deepak, this fight could have been yours as well! Anjana and I would have appreciated your stance on it while trying to learn better. What do you say, Anjana?"

'I agree with you, Panditji. One needs to learn how to take a stand in life." Then she continued, looking at Deepak, "If you have conviction about something, drive the world to believe in it. We have a lot of issues with our kids marrying outside our clan or if they opt for love marriage. But ultimately, it is your life!"

This was music to Deepak's ears. He pinched himself as he felt that what he had just heard was too good to be true. Maybe he did not understand his parents well or he took them as ultra-conservative, while all this time they were walking the distance to meet the younger generation, trying to understand their thoughts. It was possibly their way of bridging the generation gap. While Deepak got slightly lost in his thoughts, Anjana looked at him, and said a little louder than she normally did, "Deepak, you are destined to become what you want to become. So, prove us wrong. Change our perspective and get your girl! We would keep our end of the bargain, as a fighter who lost a battle."

Panditji got up from the table and went towards the powder room to wash his hands. Anjana took his plate and gave it to Kul to put in the wash basin. Kul had finished his dinner by then, so he collected the plates and all the other dishes from the dining table and took it to the wash area for cleaning. It was Kul's and Deepak's duty to clean the plates at night, alternatively. The day Deepak cleaned the utensils, Kul put up the mosquito net in all the beds, and vice-versa. The city faced a menace of mosquitoes, and while the municipal areas still got some help from the government (in the form of fogging every alternate day), the remote areas were badly infested. One had to be prepared to sleep without much air inside the net, but at least it was peaceful without the mosquitoes.

Suddenly, Panditji came back into the dining room, and announced, "If either of you can convince me to believe in love marriage or about working in Delhi despite your mother's warnings, beginning from the first of the upcoming month, I would support you wholeheartedly. But first, you must fight a battle with me and change my opinion."

Anjana added quickly, "We have cast the dice and the game is on. Take up the challenge. Provide us with thoughtful and sound arguments to change our opinion. Help us understand you and bless your actions."

Deepak could finally see some light at the end of the tunnel. He knew he had to fight the battle to get approval for his marriage with Guria. He thought about it for a bit, and left that fight for another day.

He went to the room that he and his brother shared. They both had a camp cot to themselves. It was a decent-sized room, and the siblings had a table and a chair each for their studies.

They lived in a small 2BHK house in an upmarket location in Patna, near Boring Road. They had been living there for a couple of years. Panditji had purchased this house after saving money for over twenty years of his service. It was a small complex with only six apartments, but it had a small games room where they would generally go to play carrom or cards.

Kul went to the games room while Deepak stayed back saying he had a lot of work to do. He wished to have a chat with Guria and plan his next move. He adjusted his camp cot a bit, changed the bed sheet, put on a new pair of pillow covers and took his cot closer to the window. His room had two small windows, one at the head of Deepak's cot and the other at Kul's. Deepak looked outside the window, saw the city almost asleep, with no real movement on the roads beneath, while the streetlights danced their various shades that evening, in the cool breeze.

Deepak pulled his blanket up to his chin, rubbed his hands a bit to give himself some warmth, and thought of

Guria. Ah! He awaited those beautiful winter nights when his beloved would cozy up to him for warmth and for bliss. He found her the most charming personality he had ever met. She could make his heart skip with her unusual laugh—which was at times high-pitched and sometimes in lower tones, but in a rhythm so dramatic that he called her his 'laughing nightingale'. Guria had a captivating personality and a pure heart, or at least that was what Deepak thought of her.

He thought it was better to speak to her than to keep thinking about her, as that would keep him up all night, with no respite to his longing for her. It was going to be a long night.

Chapter 4
1975

Panditji, the jailor, came in with a troupe of six guards who were armed to their teeth. All the prisoners fell in order, towards the back. The Professor was standing in front of Panditji and his police team. Behind the Professor, were Rajendra and the Shayar, Farooqui. Panditji was rather agitated as he walked in, but when he saw the three of them holding forth, he sported a wry smile on his face. He told his guards to go outside and wait for him. He then spoke in a soft and low voice to the Professor. It was difficult even for Rajendra and the Shayar to hear them. Panditji exited the room, slow but sure-footed.

The Professor turned to Rajendra and the Shayar and told them that it was the task of the three of them to manage the thirty-seven crooks in their barrack. If anyone was found involved in any activity, the entire barrack would be punished. The Shayar sounded a bit taken aback by the proposal. He felt it would be impossible for the three of them to control those goons. He knew that they would get in further trouble, sooner than later. Professor realised what was going on in his mind and addressed the inmates.

"I am Professor Dhiraj Sahay. I was going to share my introduction before all this happened. I hope you all know what transpired between Panditji and me. If not, let me make it clear to all of you. We, as a barrack of forty inmates, are going to support one another and stay out of trouble." Suddenly he heard a banging sound from behind. Someone had fallen on the floor trying to look at the Professor while listening to him. He was short in height and there were taller inmates in front of him. The Professor called him near, asked him if he was okay, and then resumed, "The atmosphere outside is sad and volatile. We cannot give any more trouble to the jailor and his force. If we cannot keep our house in order, we are in for a lot of pain and only God can save us. However, if all of you promise to work together with the three of us, we are going to keep you out of direct trouble from the authorities. What do you say?" he said, and looked at the bigger guys, who could possibly be the head crooks and order givers. Then he looked at the others with a glint in his eyes, purposefully and with a commanding posture. That he was lanky and short did not make him any less of a tall personality. His knowledge, sense of purpose, and his vision made him a towering figure.

The bigger crooks agreed to the Professor's proposal and then the others followed. All of them joined forces with the MISA group of inmates, to unite in keeping themselves out of trouble and to do something good in their lives. They knew that the Professor would help them evolve and probably reform to become respectable humans. Despite being new, he had saved an inmate from thrashing by the police within the hour of his joining. Witnessing that made them trust the Professor's belief in equality and his genuine concern for the well-being of the barrack.

The Shayar said, "I agree with the Professor, let's behave and reform ourselves for the good." His voice was soft and sonorous. It almost felt like he would render his couplets then and there.

Rajendra went ahead and congratulated the Professor, "We are up for the task at hand! We would work together for the betterment of every soul in the barrack. After prison, we can lend a helping hand as well. Somehow, both the Shayar and I have been out of trouble with the authorities until now, as we have just been here for a few days. But we have witnessed the other inmates suffer from the forces's brutality. Although we also understand that the forces are dealing with a lot currently because of the changing political scenario of the country. So, we should give them some space."

It was a happy entry for the Professor. He had made friends in his cell early on and hoped to bring a positive change in the lives of his peers.

The Professor was guided to a cot that he could use to lie down. It was his first day in, and he had to be guided by the others. It would take some time for him to get to know everyone. By that time, however, not only his cellmates, but the police would also know him well. They had their own expectations from him, and he knew that meeting them would initially spare him unnecessary trouble.

He sat down at his cot, and others quickly went back to theirs. The Professor knew that it would be a long-haul in the prison, as people under MISA were not allowed to go back to their homes quickly. They were not put in front of the Magistrates and there was no question of any bail. They were there at the whims and fancies of the police and the other authorities.

The Shayar and Rajendra walked up to the Professor.

"That was some entry, sir! It was akin to Amitabh Bachchan walking in as an Inspector in the movie, *Zanjeer*," said Rajendra.

"Frankly speaking, this went better than I thought. However, let's try and keep it this way. We must avoid trouble and focus on self-learning and self-growth."

They eventually went out for lunch to the hall where the Professor was told that he would meet other MISA prisoners, as well as the regular ones. It was a large lunch hall and they could see the prisoners in a queue, waiting for their food. Suddenly, someone came forward with a newspaper and announced,

"Mrs. Indira Gandhi's election from Rae-Bareilly has been invalidated by the respected Justice Jagmohanlal

Sinha. He delivered his verdict the day before yesterday and has barred her from another election for the next six years!"

People looked at him intently. There was murmuring in the hall. One could smell rice and bread. Prisoners lined in the queue moved forward and they were given rice, pulses, a vegetable, bread, and eggs. There was no colour in the vegetable, and the pulses were lighter than the normal home cooked ones. The pulses were watery, and looked devoid of turmeric.

Rajendra panted, adjusted his stance, held his palm on his potbelly, and said, "All praise to Justice Sinha and to our forefathers who designed this constitution. The powers of the Executive, the Legislature, and the Judiciary have been well defined and separated. What the senior government officials would do now is the question." He looked supremely excited with the prospects of a major change in the composition of the government.

Slowly, a substantial crowd gathered around Rajendra, Professor, and Umar and started listening to the conversation. Someone shouted slogans against the party in power at the centre, and the others joined in. The atmosphere inside the lunch hall was electric and the political prisoners were enthused by the verdict. It was an indication that the prime minister would probably have to relinquish governance and handover her position in favour of some other politician. Post-lunch hour, the prisoners assembled in the lawns. They wanted to know more about the verdict. Word of mouth travels fast. The MISA gang from across the barracks felt electric. They thought their troubles would soon end. They harboured apprehensions though, and wanted a discussion on the verdict with someone who understood it well. Some of them saw the police battalion with batons in their hands, slowly moving towards the crowd. The Shayar saw it and shouted at the top of his voice to get back to the barracks. There was a slight confusion, and before everyone could understand, a baton hit one of the inmates. The crowd soon dispersed. The Inmates went back to the barracks, mostly unharmed. Later, word travelled, and the guy who got struck, was declared okay. He was hit rather softly. The police had wanted to only disperse the crowd without much ado.

Inside the barrack, the Professor said to the inmates, "We must stay out of trouble. Jailor saheb is doing his best, as you can see. He is not vindictive, but he must maintain law and order at this hour of extreme political churn. Please be calm." Someone asked the meaning of the verdict, upon which the Professor said, "Hopefully, our beloved prime minister will agree with the judgment and there would not be any constitutional crisis on our hands. We are a new Republic, and we cannot see ugly fights at that level." Everyone looked at the Professor with inquisitiveness as they listened to his pearls of wisdom, and the Professor understood that they were with him, and that he could keep them safe. The Professor looked at Rajendra *ji* for his inputs.

Rajendra ji took the cue and said, "Well, presuming the current prime minister relinquishes her post in the government and moves to the party, that would still be a below par change than what this crowd wished for." Everyone agreed that they were seeking a total revolution, a total change in the way India was being run and managed, and they wanted the opposition parties to take over the governance. This possible change of guard would be the death knell of an empire, or so they thought.

There were close to two hundred political prisoners in the prison. They hailed from a good stratum of the society, from different parts of Bihar, and all of them believed in JP's (Jai Prakash Narain's) call for a complete revolution. They knew that JP could take the country on the right path and create a change as was desired during the freedom struggle.

At that moment, they saw the jailor walking towards them with an entourage of ten policemen, carrying batons. The entire barrack suddenly became silent.

Panditji came near them and said, "Professor Saheb, they were going to sound the *pagli ghanti* today. They would have taken all of you to task. I initially told them to just disperse the crowd outside the lunch hall. We saw the crowd dispersed quickly. Of course, you guys are of great help, but inside your barrack also, let there be life as usual. No congregations, and no hate speeches please."

The Professor nodded at the jailor and said, "I would do all in my power to keep it quiet inside this barrack. I agree with you. There is a huge political flux and things might take an ugly turn. We will practice strict compliance with the rules of the jail and exercise discipline."

Panditji wore a tense look which was quite different from his usual beaming face, as attested to by Rajendra and the Shayar. They knew things could go squarely wrong for them within a matter of minutes.

The Professor got the cue and asked everyone to keep quiet and not raise any sort of slogans. He did not want the police to go berserk and *lathi*-charge them. It was a momentous occasion, alright, but he asked everyone to speak quietly amongst themselves and seek information through the newspapers. The country was changing, and everyone was excited. They all wanted a piece of the pie and they were entitled to it as well, as they had given up their freedom for it.

They wished for a new dawn.

Chapter 5
1973

"Yes, I wanted to meet you and have dinner together. Hence the hurry. I hope you understand." Deepak got up from his seat and gave Guria a small, almost formal hug. They were in a restaurant near Guria's house. It was a casual dining restaurant and offered decent food with some good mocktails. Deepak quickly ordered some food for the two of them and checked with Guria if she craved for any particular mocktail. Guria ordered a chilli infused litchi drink for herself while she ordered a masala coke for Deepak.

"What has changed, Deepak? Why are you behaving so differently? Why are you being so... so formal? Are you going to break-up with me tonight?" Guria asked.

"Absolutely not! I cannot even think of that. I have not changed, Guria. But we must grow up," Deepak said in a slightly elevated tone.

"I get it, Deepak. I feel good whenever I come here with you. Remember, this was the joint we came to for our first official date?" Guria smirked, pouted a bit, and made the air a little lighter between them. She got up from her chair and stood next to Deepak who had a startled look on his face. He wanted to get up as well thinking Guria wished to leave the restaurant that instant. She, however, patted him to relax in his seat and gave him a side hug. Deepak had a broad smile on his face and Guria had warmth and affection writ all over hers. She wanted Deepak to tell her about the conversation regarding the Delhi job right there, but did not want to push him too much. He looked stressed but she was confident that Deepak loved her and that he would do everything possible to marry her.

As they ate, they made some small talk before Deepak finally told her about his entire conversation with his parents and his mother's predictions. Guria sounded disheartened at the turn of events.

"I am shocked, Deepak! Would you really agree to her demand? Forgive me for saying this, but it seems so foolish. How can someone not go in a particular direction for two years? Did she know that you were planning to go to Delhi? Does she know about us?" Guria asked, anxiously.

"Don't get upset, Guria. I believe in my mother's palmistry skills. She learned it from my *Nanaji* who was very famous for the same. There are instances in our family's past where she has guided us out of danger by forecasting and pre-empting it," saying thus, Deepak held Guria's palms. They had an unwritten chemistry between them. They had known each other for a couple of years, and they had fond memories together. They were friends first and lovesick adults later. Guria squeezed Deepak's hands, moved them towards herself, and kissed him on his palms. It melted the tension in the air and Deepak felt a bit relaxed. The food was delicious, and she knew he would love it. She nodded in agreement for Deepak to continue, and he said, "I believe she knows something that is not good at all. She also says there is no ring or chant that she could teach me to ward off the danger. The best course now is to avoid going north, even to the northern side of Patna. Let me also tell you, she did not know about my job offer when she told me about this prediction, nor is she aware of our relationship. She did ask me though if I had a girlfriend. I did not answer her on that."

"Oh Deepak, that is quite some information to process. Okay, so what's the plan now?"

"Well, I was thinking of dropping the idea of going to Delhi. Mummy told me that I could get a job in some other large trading firm in Patna which would offer me a good salary as well. So, I would have to find that job for myself as soon as possible."

"That is brilliant! I think aunty is a rockstar. I was going to tell you today itself about a job in an agricultural trading firm in Patna. It is a well-paying job for the position of marketing executive. Would you like to apply for it? Can you meet them tomorrow?"

"I can meet them tomorrow. Let me know the appointment details and I would be there on time. May I know how you know the owners?"

"Listen, you just concentrate on the interview. You are a talented guy, and I hope and pray that you get this job. That way we can continue to be together, here in Patna. We can figure out our marriage plans later," Guria said and held Deepak's hand in both her palms.

Deepak looked at Guria with a soft look on his face. He felt as though she was his *Vighnaharta*. He had a tear in his left eye, which he smartly removed saying something had gone inside his eye. All this while, Guria smiled at him. She felt that he was cute and a good person. Deepak knew that Guria was the one person who knew exactly how and when to take over his troubles and provide adequate and working solutions. He was sure that she would make a fantastic life-partner. He knew he had to start fighting for his rights and back himself on his choices. He needed to speak to his mom and tell her all about Guria. Anjana might be resourceful, for all he knew. She might even tell him a way to overcome the issue of caste and get an approval from Panditji. He decided to give it a shot. However, first things first, he needed to get the job within the week. He would then initiate the conversation about Guria at home.

They finished their dinner and then Deepak took her to a nearby ice-cream parlour. He ordered a *pista kulfi* for her and an orange flavoured ice-cream for himself. They spoke about their time in the college. Guria giggled through the conversation, while Deepak exuded a silent charm. Guria thought it was difficult to find such a charming, mature, and decent gentleman in Patna. She was a doting beloved, love-struck and could morph into any being that moment to hug him. He did not like hugs in public and she was aware of it. Even holding hands made him cringe and she had accepted him as he was.

Left to herself, she would have had his ice-cream from his mouth, right there in front of the parlour, but she knew he was most disapproving of public displays of affection. Despite his reservations, she gave her kulfi to Deepak, who held it in his hands, looking at Guria hogging on his ice-cream. She admonished him for not having the melting kulfi, which he devoured thereafter. Guria paid the parlour bill, and they went towards the bike. She hurried in front of him and sat on the bike's seat, facing him. He looked a bit surprised, but she made it clear she needed some time with him before they went back home.

They spoke about how they used to be in different groups during college. Deepak was in a group of pupils good at mathematics and sciences, while she was in the commerce group. They were somehow acquainted to each other, but hardly met as they had separate classes. They spent some time together in a college fete, as providence had it that one of the commerce students had his sister in Deepak's group. They got together for the day, playing and working together. They had their evening tea and dinner together that evening, exhausted as they were after a long day. They had an instant chemistry, and while they were different in mannerisms and in their pocket money, Deepak found her to be charming and a glib talker, while Guria found him to be gentlemanly. Till her college days, she had not met someone of his type. He was her age, but he was mature quite unlike a rustic local, he spoke well, and had a brooding personality, with his height and his looks. For Deepak, Guria was a breath of fresh air. Her smile and her constant chatter were heavenly for him. They met often on some pretext or the other in college, did not say they liked each other, but the relationship grew. Guria knew that Deepak was off-limits for her as far as any sexual advances were concerned. He believed at best in a quick hug, a peck on the cheeks when she would demand, or a normal kiss on the forehead. His hands would start and stop at her palms. She had to sometimes tickle him for him to tickle her back. That was all they had done over the years of their romantic relationship. Guria wanted a bit more at times, at least a good lip-to-lip kiss, but she knew that that would make Deepak awkward and probably destroy their relationship. He wanted to take it slowly, and only after marriage. Guria had to make do with the seeming proximity over the phone call at night, post dinner, when their families went to sleep.

Guria stayed in a bungalow off Boring Road. It was a large white bungalow, more like a mansion of the rich and famous of the city. Deepak dropped Guria to her bungalow, and kissed her goodbye on her forehead, saying, "I love you and I will do everything in my power to be with you for life. Don't worry!" Guria was visibly happy, she held him by his hands, caressed his forearm for a moment, had a tinkle in her eyes, and kissed him on his lips gently. Deepak felt a bit awkward, looked around to check if anyone saw them, forced a smile on his discoloured face, and went away towards his own flat in the same vicinity. His flat was smaller, but a good one with basic amenities.

Guria's thoughts were in his mind, but he knew he must prepare for his big day.

Chapter 6

1975

"Jailor Saheb, please join us for tea," Rajendra Agarwal invited Panditji to their group of three.

"Rajendra Babu, please call me Panditji. I am comfortable that way amongst friends and family. I love interacting with you guys and we could be part of a *chandaal chowkdi.*" He got his big frame to accommodate itself somehow on the available chair, tweaked his hair a bit, exercised his fingers as if he were making dough, and said, "My only issue is that I cannot make it official and well known to others as I am on government duty. However, I can have tea with you."

"We are quite anxious to know what is happening outside in our country now. We request you to share some highlights. Please tell us your perspective also," the Professor requested.

"Be fearless, sir, and tell us. The heart is writhing,

please let us know the situation of our country," the Shayar said in his quintessential style.

"Well, I do not wish to share my personal viewpoint on the current events. However, what we do understand is that the way things are moving in the country politically, we have evidence to believe that the democracy could be in grave danger. I am not allowed to utter any of these words, but I can depend upon the three of you to have my back on this." He looked at his three friends, who nodded in agreement, and having been reassured, he began, "There is a growing uneasiness within the ruling party as to what route the Prime Minister would take. She does not have much of a choice within the existing constitution, so she might not want to create a constitutional crisis by defying a High Court order." He took a sip of tea, enlarged his eyes, gesticulated, and commented further, "The Prime Minister is innovative, sharp and has the nerves of steel. People expect the worst to happen going ahead." Panditji had chewed on the available information to give his answer.

"Well, people believe her to be pragmatic and honourable. She should relinquish her chair in favour of an able leader. She should also consider continuing to work for her party for the time being and keep in touch with the people of the country. I don't think she would take any step in a haste," the Professor had a point which the others agreed to, but he added, "She would carefully consider all the alternatives and then choose the path of least resistance."

"I choose to disagree with you, Professor Saheb. You are being passionate, or might I say partial, in your judgement of the Prime Minister. The times have changed. People have become corrupt," Rajendra opined. He then took a sip of tea, and continued, "We are not in the year 1942 or 1947. You speak as if every single politician in our country has a deep conscience, and they would only do good for the society. But that is sadly not true. Get real! I think she will take the path of maximum resistance and push her weight through. She would willingly take risks to stay put. That is my reading of the politicians in general and I speak from experience. Our honourable Prime Minister is feisty and strong. She would take her risks."

"*Arz kiya hai*," the Shayar raised his right hand to speak, and the others promptly said, "*Irshaad*!" and he continued,

"Zarre zarre se buland ek awaz aayi hai,
Zarre – zarre se buland ek awaz aayi hai;
Kursi ki deewangi parwaan chadhegi,
Kya yeh wahi ehsaas layi hai?"

(A loud call comes from each particle of my being,
A loud call comes from each particle of my being.
The lust for power will reach its zenith,
Has it brought that same feeling?)

"Wow, awesome!" the others exclaimed in unison in appreciation of the couplet.

"*Adab arz hai*!" the Shayar said.

"*Tasleem!*" the Professor replied.

"Oh, I'm happy to see that you guys are learning a bit of Urdu! That is interesting. But, Professor, you have not responded to Rajendra *bhai* yet."

"Farooqui saheb, it seems he has already chosen his side in this discussion," Panditji blurted out.

"I sincerely hope that all of you are incorrect in your present assessments. If she takes any other path, there could be mayhem. We could be in for a huge change. It would be out of the ordinary and we could be pushed into being a failed democracy, akin to Pakistan. I hope that does not happen," the Professor said, and the others had to agree with him.

They would speak again on the subject, but they were waiting for some more news. Those were uneasy times. A nation state was in a crisis and the present dispensation had to save it before it got too late. People awaited the next steps of the country's top leadership. They wanted to see whether the government would go on a war with the judiciary, or if the top leadership would back down and allow the constitutional process to continue. There was a spring in the steps of the common man, he thought that the country was likely to undergo a positive change in the government leadership. They also felt that there was a chance the Opposition could take over governance of the country, thereby giving hope to the masses. For the masses, one must understand, the need was limited to *roti, kapda aur makaan*. All they wanted was to get out of the below poverty line into the middle class, and be able to afford the luxuries of a normal life. They wanted the inflation to reduce, food to be made available at lower rates, have a proper shelter, and the police atrocities to be reined in. They wanted their government to hear their voices and provide for their minimal requirements. They wanted jobs and they were willing to fight to the finish.

Chapter 7

1971

"Simdega has never seen a show like this before. What a performance by Professor Saheb!"

"What an amazing coordination of light and sound. It was mesmerising."

"The way he has been able to fuse technology with his voice-over and the effort that has been put in managing a thousand students over the last hour is commendable, to say the least."

"It calls for a celebration—a celebration of a director par excellence."

"Had he been in Mumbai, he would have made a fine director of Bollywood films. His voice is apt for the All India Radio," someone in the crowd said to the person next to him.

Murmurings were happening in the Simdega College grounds where a crowd of almost five thousand citizens of the small town had gathered.

Someone else said, “Teachers like him create pupils who go above and beyond in their careers. This show was beyond our wildest imagination.”

Another person said to the one next to him, “I am sure that the evening is only going to get better. I have some *litti-chokha* with me. Would you want to eat a couple of them while we wait for the Shayar to come to the stage?” The person next to him was delighted to be offered litti-chokha during the program, that too by an unknown, kind-hearted person.

The crowd held their breaths as they had just seen the ‘Quit India Movement’ in light and sound on the occasion of the silver jubilee of the Indian independence. The anticipation only grew with the wait getting longer for Farooqui saheb to take the stage. Finally, the Professor saheb came on to the stage to announce the entry of the Shayar, Umar Farooqui.

“I hope you had a good time watching the light and sound show.” He looked towards the crowd in front of him and got a standing ovation.

“I am pleased with your response. We did not leave any stone unturned for this event. Now, I would like to invite my dear friend and a great mentor, Shayar Umar Farooqui to the stage.”

He saw Farooqui saheb walking up to the stage. The Shayar was welcomed with loud cheers and claps by the crowd. The Professor hugged him and brought him forward, towards the microphone.

"Our friendship goes long back. I have known him as a mentor over the last ten years. That he is a great performer, none of us have any doubt about, but he also has a mesmerising personality and is a humble soul. The more you meet him, the more you will appreciate him. And now, without any further ado, I would leave the stage to our esteemed performer for the evening—Shayar Umar Farooqui!" saying this, the Professor left the stage.

"Professor saheb has given me a lot of respect. I wish to thank him from the bottom of my heart."

The Shayar waited for a moment for the crowd to settle down and then began, "Arz kiya hai…" he said and waited as the crowd said in unison, "Irshaad, irshaad."

"It is the mercy of the Lord, the Professor has been so blessed; How can I not share my thoughts, the Professor has requested me."

The crowd cheered, "*Subhan-allah!* Tasleem*!*"

The Shayar continued,

"Haal-e-dil kya bayan karun,
Tabassum sa ik chehra dekha tha,
Sadiyan beet gayi, ab toh chehre bhi daagdaar se ho chale hain,
Gandhi ji ne jo azaadi ka khwaab dikhaya tha, woh aaj bhi adhoora hai
Gila karein kinse hum, jub dukhon ka Farroqui par saaya hai,
Miya Farooqui gareeb nahin hain dil se,
Yeh aazmaish kar lo ai parvardigar,

Hum se yeh dil hamara maang kar dekho,
Dariyadili ka hum ab bhi shauk rakhte hain,
Hum zaar-zaar ro rahe hain, ai-watan tujhe yeh kya hua hai,
Hum zaar-zaar ro rahe hain ai-watan;
Aisi garibi toh humne na socha tha aazadi ke baad hum-watanon ko milegi,
Miya Farooqui ki guzaarish hai, wazir-e-azam se,
Hum-watanon ko do waqt ki roti dene mein teri pareshaani ka sabab ab kuch ruasa kar jaata hai.
Ae-watan ke rakhwalon, kya humne yeh kabhi socha tha,
Ik woh bhi din aayega, jab humari aulad hamein kosegi ek pyala doodh ke liye,
Yeh kis dharti par tumne hamein aab-o-daana diya ae waleed,
Miya Farooqui sharmsar hai, Miya Farooqui sharmsar hai
Teri bandagi mein baitha hai, kuch toh bayan kar ae khuda!"

(What thoughts can I share,
I had seen a smiling face;
Decades have passed by, and the beautiful faces have also lost sheen,
Gandhi ji had shown us dreams of freedom, but they remain incomplete;
With whom can I share my misgivings when I myself am caught in a rut,

I am not poor by heart;
Ask what you have to, from me oh Lord,
Ask from me, my heart;
I still possess the trait of being generous,
I cry for my country's well-being, I do not know what has happened to our great nation;
I cry O great nation,
We never thought this kind of poverty would be there in our country for our brethren;
I request our Prime Minister,
We feel sad to see you in deep thoughts and to see your inability to feed the poor millions of our country;
The gatekeepers of our country, did we ever think earlier of such times,
We will see a day where our children will look at us with disgrace as we are not even able to feed them milk;
Why did you bring us into this world, in this country, O father,
I feel shameful,
I sit at your prayer, waiting to hear from you, O Lord!)

The Shayar raised his right hand and folding it slightly inward, motioned towards the crowd as he slowly said, "Adab arz hai."

The crowd went hysterical. They just loved the *nazm* delivered soulfully by the Shayar. It brought out the inner voice of every Indian citizen. The people were hurt and concerned about the daily increase in prices of basic commodities. People were taking out loans from their provident funds to buy rice, wheat, and oil. Inflation control had become impossible for the country's premier bank, The Reserve Bank of India. And amidst all this, they could see that the representative powers were concentrated on securing their own political positions.

Be it electricity, water supply, homes for the homeless, clothes for the unclothed, or food for the hungry, it seemed as though no one was interested in giving the basic rights to the common populace. The people were counting their blessings post-independence, as they wished to see a powerful and rich India once again. Why was that thought slowly petering away? Nobody had any answers. They looked towards the politicians, the judges, and the journalists for answers, but none had any. The common man had been converted into a vote-bank for various political parties. They were being mocked by the same politicians for their ignorance. Their dignity was being snatched away from them, whilst they stood in various queues to fulfil the basic demands of their ever-increasing families. These were tough times for a fast-changing nation and the common man sought answers.

The crowd at the Simdega College grounds just went wild as they related to every word of the Shayar's nazm and wanted to meet him in person. So, a small group of students appeared on the stage and frisked him away.

It was an entertaining evening by all counts for the crowd at Simdega. They were more than happy with the organisers and Professor saheb. Soon, the night approached, and the crowd thinned out considerably. The

Shayar accompanied the Professor to his residence. They reached there quite late, but a sumptuous dinner cooked by Nilima, the Professor's wife, was waiting for them. Their children had already eaten dinner and gone to bed. Nilima was elated to meet the Shayar and they had an hour-long impromptu session of *sher-o-shayari* at the dining table. Nilima had cooked mutton with *naan* and *raita*, salad. She was a student of history but was also quite proficient in the Hindi language and literature. She was also a very good singer, and upon the Professor's repeated requests, she sang a couple of songs.

They spent the next day together as well. The Shayar was pleased to meet the Professor's kids, Niru, and Rohit. They were four and two years old and he enjoyed playing with them. The Shayar and his wife were not blessed with any children, and he always perceived that deprivation as God's way of leaving him asking for more. That afternoon, he took a bus to Ranchi, having had a feast for lunch, for which the Professor's neighbour had also been invited. It was a hearty meal and all of them had a blast.

Nilima later spoke to the Professor about God's will. She was into prayers and mediation, and said that she would pray for the well-being of the Shayar.

The Professor was not happy with how the country was being governed, and he had started speaking openly about it in various forums. Nilima regularly counselled him against being so openly critical of the government, as he was the only breadwinner of the family. She was a homemaker, and his larger family was in Ranchi.

For the Professor, however, it was about truth and destiny. He would often give the response that, if in the fight for truth and justice, he had to lose his job or to go to jail, or if his family had to move to Ranchi under the fold of their grandparents, it would be acceptable to him.

Nilima was worried. She knew that her husband had the mindset of a revolutionary, and he was a well-known figure in their small town. It would be very easy for the local administration to pick him up and make an example out of him. He could be put behind bars for anti-government activities and could lose his job in the bargain as well. The Professor consoled her by saying that nothing would happen to him. However, if anything were to happen and if it were in his destiny, she had to be brave enough to shift to Ranchi.

Nilima had slowly prepared herself for it. She knew that if something like that happened to her husband, she had to rise to the occasion and take all the necessary steps to secure her and her children's safety and survival. The Professor had got her introduced to the principal of his college, saying that he would help Nilima deal with any issues that may crop up.

Nilima was a gutsy young lady.

Chapter 8

1973

"Babu," Guria called out to her father, Rajendra Agarwal. "Breakfast is ready. Please come. I'm famished. Mummy, please get Amit too. I am starting. I can't wait when there is *poori* and *aloo dum* on the table!"

"Guria, what is the matter? Are you going out somewhere? You have already taken a bath and performed puja early this morning!" Chitra, Guria's mother exclaimed.

"No, Mummy. I am very much at home today. I just wanted to speak to Babu this morning before he goes out for the day."

'Oh, so something important, I suppose. What is the matter, *beta*?" Chitra asked.

"Sit down, Mummy. I'll tell you. It is something important as it has to do with my future. It's about Deepak and my relationship with him..." just as Guria completed her sentence, Rajendra walked in for his breakfast.

"Tell me also about your future, beta? What's the matter? All decked up early in the morning. Oh, I love *poori-bhaji*. Thank you, *memsaab*!" Rajendra winked at Chitra, and she waved her hands rather timorously in response.

"Babu," Guria said. "Deepak will come to meet you at your office today at twelve thirty. He does not know that you are my dad. Interview him and give him the marketing executive's job that you were hiring for. He is not going to Delhi to join the MNC firm. His mother did not allow him to go as she feels it would harm his interests. She is a palmist, and she does not want him to travel to anywhere north for the next couple of years."

"Which son listens to his mother so much nowadays? This guy is evidently different. You would keep him under your thumb, it seems." Rajendra looked at Guria and almost goaded her to tell him more about Deepak.

"No, Babu. he is a man of substance. He does not take any hasty decisions. He does not intend to hurt his parents or, for that matter, anyone. He behaves nicely with me too. He wants to marry me, but first, he wishes to settle down. He is going to have a talk with his father about us after that happens."

"Okay, beta, I will give him the job. All I am worried about is you and no one else. You have given away your heart to a guy who does not speak to his parents about your relationship, and they belong to a different caste as well. I just don't want to see you in trouble in the future. Also, this plan about him working for me without knowing about my relationship with you, have you thought about it thoroughly? From what I perceive, this kind of a guy would not like to work in his to-be father-in-law's firm; that too without knowing that he has gotten the job at the behest of his girlfriend. It could blow up in your face later."

"Babu, I have thought it through. I will manage, don't worry. I can't thank you enough! Here, take one more poori," Guria said, elated.

Amit, Guria's brother, came out of the bathroom hurriedly and went to the table.

"You are again late, Amit. Look, your *didi* is decked up just to be at home. Why don't you take her somewhere with you? Go for a movie or something," Chitra suggested.

"*Mumma*, she would not come with me to a movie. All she wants to do is spend time in a mall, window shopping. She has no agenda while shopping and I don't like that. One should have clarity of purpose while visiting a mall. Take the items you wish to buy, have some food and drinks, and get going! She will never understand that!" Amit complained.

Chitra, Guria, and Rajendra laughed at his words. Amit served himself and ate quickly, as was getting late to go to his friends' house.

They were a close-knit family and liked being in each other's company.

Guria was delighted as Deepak was about to get his job that day. She hoped that he would speak to his parents about their marriage after that. She looked forward to getting married to him and she knew providence would have it that way. She felt that the Almighty would listen to her sincere call for help. She was in love, more than ever, and she could feel a glow on her skin. She was simple yet elegant, but she was amazed at nature's way of glamming her up. She felt on top of the world in love, and hoped to get what she deserved.

Chapter 9
1975

"Professor saheb, it has been an eventful month. The Supreme Court has only given a conditional stay to the application of our Prime Minister and has effectively disallowed her voting rights. Where is this leading to? What would JP do now? He has organised a mass event today at Delhi, in the lion's den. It is being called '*Sampoorna Kranti*'. What do you think would happen? Will Mrs. Gandhi resign now? Or will she wait it out till either the final decision of the Supreme Court or the next elections in 1976?" Rajendra Agarwal asked.

"It's difficult to predict her moves. She has a battery of lawyers working for her, like Nani Palkhivala. Siddhartha Shankar Ray, the Chief Minister of West Bengal, is also helping her." The Professor enjoyed such discussions over a cup of piping hot tea. He drank his tea, almost twenty times a day, when at home or at his college.

Here, however, he had tea only twice a day. Tea was his favourite beverage. He did not take any hard drinks.

He continued, "Madam Prime Minister is a feisty person. She will take the fight to the finish. She will not give up. JP will not relent either. He is a Gandhian and one of the tallest freedom fighters of our country." The Professor eyes showed a deep reverence while speaking. "His work with Vinoba Bhave through the years has been exemplary. This is a massive fight and something big is going to happen soon. But I cannot predict what."

The Shayar raised his hands slowly, requesting to be allowed to add his two bits to the discussion, and upon being approved of the same, hastened to say, "One must read the constitution carefully to understand the possible outcomes. Some of the journals recently have mentioned that our Honourable Prime Minister could proclaim a national emergency."

Taking the cue from the discussion, Rajendra added, "The Prime Minister could use the present law and order situation and proclaim an Emergency. It is highly unlikely though, as it would be a dark day for our democracy. What do you think, Shayar Farooqui?"

"Wazir-e-azam se kya khafa ho, samay hi kuch naraz sa hai,
Jamhooriyat khatre mein hai Farooqui, aur apne bhi begaane se lagne lage hain;
Khud ko tum sambhal lena, ahle-vatan, zamaana kharaab hai."

(We should not be upset with the Prime Minister
when the time itself is not right,
Our democracy is in grave danger Farooqui, and our
own people seem like strangers;
My country, save yourself, as times are not good.)

"Are you saying that there is no reason to be angry at the Prime Minister as time itself has gone awry and as democracy is in danger, our own people seem unknown to us and therefore, one must take care of one's own self?" the Professor asked, summing up the import of the Shayar's couplet.

"You will soon start writing couplets in Urdu yourself, Professor saheb. Your grasp of Urdu couplets deserves much praise."

"Oh God, you guys have taken a normal conversation to a poetic level. Can we just talk about the state of our country?" Rajendra lightly admonished the other two. I agree with Professor saheb. In certain instances, the Indian constitution does allow for the declaration of an Emergency. The Prime Minister may move the resolution in a cabinet meeting and forward the recommendation to the President."

The Professor interjected, saying, "They could make a case of rioting, damage to the institutions, and complete breakdown of law and order in the country. If you remember, JP has already called for a Sampoorna Kranti. He has gone ahead and called out the police and the army to act as per their conscience and not follow any direct orders."

Panditji added to the discussion saying, "In this situation, and with today's Delhi rally, if things go south, Mrs. Gandhi might just take that recommendation to the President. It is a likely course of action according to me." He paused for an effect, got up from his seat, moved in a semi-circle around his friends, sat down again, and said, "Let me also tell you that I do not speak as a government servant. I speak as a citizen of the country who understands the political climate well enough. At least, I would like to believe so."

"In any case, it would be indeed a dark day for the Indian democracy. It remains to be seen what will unfold. The next seventy-two hours are critical. We must hope for the best, with the best result being her resignation and a call for fresh elections. Let's go for lunch. Would you like to join us, Jailor saheb?" Rajendra asked.

"No, thank you. I will have lunch in my chamber. We will meet tomorrow again at this hour. Things may get worse going ahead. Have a good meal till you can," Panditji said, with the hint of a nervous smile on his face.

It was a restless day for the country. There was a massive rally organised at the Ramlila Maidan in Delhi. Lakhs of people attended the rally to hear the likes of Atal Behari Vajpayee, Morarji Desai, and Jai Prakash Narain. JP read out poet Dinkar's lines,

"Singhasan khali karo ke Janata aati hai."

(Step down from governance as people come to take direct charge.)

It was a massive show of strength by a united Opposition. JP called for the resignation of Mrs. Gandhi and reiterated his call to the Army and Police about disregarding immoral and unconstitutional orders. The call for a constitutional crisis may have led to the impeding decision on declaring an Emergency. Chaos writ large and the country faced its first major constitutional crisis. The Commoners were growing ecstatic with the developments reported on a daily basis. With limited information filtering around the country, as the Press was kept under a tight leash, word of mouth generated hysteria in the country. People expected a crackdown by the authorities, but they were also buzzing with excitement.

The Ramlila Maidan rally was organised despite a complete clampdown by the government, and it left its mark on the nation's psyche.

Chapter 10
1973

"Babu, thank you! I got a call from Deepak. He was very happy with his job offer and was surprised at your speed of execution." Guria said.

Rajendra interjected, "Yes, I have asked him to join from tomorrow itself. It was my daughter's wish, so I had to grant it," saying thus, he opened his arms for his daughter.

She hugged him, and said, "Also, Deepak was appreciative of the firm that you have built. He said that there was so much to learn from you."

"Beta, had that been true, his CV would have been routed through HR and would have never come up to me. I would have not met just any guy for an executive's role." Rajendra sat on the sofa near him, and Guria offered him a glass of water. He further said, "Just because you like him, all these rules were bent. So, we are not a very professional organisation. But anyway, I liked his knowledge and hunger for growth. He wishes to earn a lot of money, but by the right means, and seems to be a good boy. However, I would hold my judgment still for now and tell you my final opinion about him within a month or so," Guria nodded in agreement but was internally delighted.

Guria was ecstatic because soon Deepak would be working in her dad's firm, and Rajendra would teach him the ropes of the business and help his career grow. She needed to reveal the truth about this being her dad's firm at an opportune time.

Chitra saw that Guria was happy and was on her phone the entire evening. She patted her daughter and said, "Guria, can you show us a photograph of Deepak? Your Babu has already met him, but I have not. Why don't you invite him to our house someday for dinner? That way, we would also get to know each other a bit. What do you say *Guria ke papa*?"

Chitra looked at Rajendra.

"I don't have any problem with it. But she cannot invite him home until she tells him the truth about how he got his job. When are you going to do that, Guria?" Rajendra asked.

"Soon, Babu. I first want him to get settled in his job and start liking it. Then I would surely tell him the truth. Also, mummy, here are some photographs of Deepak. Look, isn't he handsome? Here, see this one, it's our photo from, I guess, a year back. We look good together, don't we?" Guria was excited and her parents were also happy for her.

Amit suddenly took the photographs away from Chitra and started running around the house while scanning through Guria and Deepak's photos. Oh, they look so funny together, Mumma! How could you, didi? He is so different. He does not even look like an adult, but a kid of my age. Look, he still does not have a stubble."

"I like him, Amit," Guria said, somehow managing to snatch the photographs back. "He is mature, and he is manly. He is also considerate. You would not understand a girl's heart. That's why you are not steady with anyone and keep getting a new girlfriend every alternate month. Mumma, tell him not to tease me!"

"Come here, Amit." Chitra said, slightly twisting Amit's ear. "Having so many girlfriends at this young age is not good. Your time will also come. But for now, concentrate on your studies, obtain good marks, and make a suitable career for yourself. If you do that, then these things will automatically follow. Oh God, Guria ke papa, why don't you say anything to this spoilt brat of yours. Were you like this yourself?" Chitra looked at Rajendra, raised her eyebrows and put up a teasing smile.

"Eh, come on! I married as per my parents' wish. Although, now I realise, I could have found a better partner for myself, had I done love marriage. These youngsters are so fortunate. They can choose their own life partner," Rajendra said and winked at Chitra.

"Babu, very funny! You would never have gotten a lovelier wife than Mumma. Grandma and grandpa did a great job in finding you such a nice woman. You are one of the few people who are happy in an arranged marriage!" Guria mentioned.

"I agree with you, Guria, but only partially. I wholeheartedly agree that she is the best wife that I could have got!" Rajendra concluded.

Chitra felt ecstatic at the thought of having a son-in-law soon. She always wanted to have Guria married into a nice family. God was great and she felt it would happen sooner than later. Suddenly they heard a commotion outside their house, on the streets. She saw a few youngsters marching on the streets, with banners and posters proclaiming independence from the tyrannical rule and establishing real democracy. She closed the doors and windows fearing some police action nearby. She felt it was unfortunate for the country to be going down the path that it was.

Chitra also felt that it would take some magic to run her household with the limited funds that her husband gave her. Internally, she wanted Guria's marriage at the earliest, and she thought of having a chat with Rajendra soon about the jewellery and other purchases they needed to do. She was a mother after all and had plans of a larger-than-life celebration during her daughter's marriage. She wanted to give her daughter, the best jewellery money could buy. It was going to be a lot of work ahead!

Chapter 11
1975

"Panditji, why is there a commotion today? Why are so many new prisoners coming in? Are they all political prisoners, arrested following the recent political developments?" the Professor asked.

"I can only guess right now, Professor saheb. We have been asked to prepare for at least a thousand new prisoners. All major leaders from the opposition parties in the city are being arrested, and they are being brought here. It seems like our honourable Prime Minister is taking some strict action. As of now, however, we are not aware of any proclamation of the Emergency. But from the looks of it though, it seems bad."

"Sinister! Unworthy of our democracy. Is it for this day that our forefathers had fought for independence? Is this *Sampoorna Swaraj*? Is this what Dr. Rajendra Prasad meant by Swaraj? Where is this country going? We have turned the clock and we will go centuries back if this continues. I think this is a preparation before announcing the Emergency," the Professor surmised.

"I would request you to keep your mouths shut and not goad anyone to shout slogans. We have very strict orders to use brutal force, if required. I hope and I pray that I can keep all of you safe." Panditji's voice had changed to dead serious. He continued, "Please follow the basic rules and decorum of this jail, and no one would get hurt. If, however, you do see some troublemakers, do not try to counsel them. Just run back to your barracks and wait there. Those troublemakers would be dealt with." Panditji had some sweat on his temple, and felt agitated, adding further, "I have deployed around fifty more policemen in this jail. I will manage the affairs strictly and will keep informing you guys of the developments. This is the fight to the finish. Let us see how it develops. Till then, goodbye and take care!" Panditji said and slowly walked away. The professor understood his message and counselled everyone in his barracks. On listening to this conversation, and upon the professor's short but effective speech inside the barracks, the Shayar lamented,

"Ae Parvardigar, ye tujhe hua kya hai,
Ye humein kis zulm ki saza de raha hai,
Yeh kambakht hosho-havaas kho baithe hain,
Kya tere dar pe is marz ki bhi koi dawa hai?"

(Oh Lord, what has happened to you,
What sin are you punishing us for,

These people have lost their sense of right and wrong,
Do you have any cure for this affliction?)

"Shayar Farooqui, the country will go through troubled times in the near future," prophesised the Professor. "We will see the limits of suppression of human rights. I don't think even the Gods would like to help the common man in today's India." The Professor was shaking while he spoke. He was infuriated at the turn of events, and wished for a change in the government at the centre. His wish was not his wish alone, it mirrored the wishes of the multitude in common people of the country at that time.

The Shayar held the Professor by his shoulder and gave him a quick side hug. The Shayar also looked vulnerable at that moment, while Rajendra and Panditji looked agitated but composed. The Professor continued, "God would also wait for things to get clearer and for either JP or Mrs. Gandhi to win this battle. We are in for tough times ahead and the Indian constitution will test its own limits. Public servants will become mere stooges and the Press would be under stiff control. Even the Judiciary will have to fight its own battle with an autocratic Executive body, and it will be a long and arduous battle. But for now, let us take it easy and try and keep the flock silent. Any misstep in this jail now will get us sent to the *kaala pani*." People could see the dark days ahead as the Professor had outlined. He was an orator and he had internalised the fight against oppression and tyranny. Panditji quietly spoke to Rajendra and to the Shayar, advising them to keep the Professor engaged in some other discussions. Panditji was responsible for keeping the three out of harm's way, being their friend and a caretaker. He was annoyed at the political scenario of the country, but was also under pressure from a severely agitated Professor. He knew he had a job at hand, and so he had to keep the Professor out of harm's way. He didn't intend to take any action against his friend.

Those were tough times and the four of them had to get out of the mess they were in, together.

Chapter 12
1973

02 March
19:40 hrs

"Deepak, my love! I'm so happy to see you after so many days. You have been so busy that it feels like you're ignoring me!". Guria hugged Deepak knowing fully well he would feel awkward about it, but she needed the hug. Deepak took a step back and Guria continued, "Just joking. You must be learning a great deal about your new job, and I hope you're liking it!" She winked at Deepak, who flushed, and she loved it. She was the naughty one and she loved to trouble Deepak, in her own loving way. Deepak loved her and knew that she took certain advantages of him, but he was okay with it. He did not understand why he became so stiff when Guria played her antics on him, but in any case, he loved her. They were at a restaurant in Boring Road, where Guria lived, and it was the evening. The restaurant was not crowded but contained a decent number of guests.

'Thanks for your help, Guria. You literally got me this job. Mr. Rajendra Agarwal, the owner of the firm, is a gentle person with a deep understanding of business. He is a self-made man, and he has an inspiring presence in the company. People respect him to the point of adoring him. He has created a firm where all the employees feel an ownership and they go beyond their duty to help the company grow." Guria took his hand in hers, as she watched him speak. Deepak was happy his beloved worked as a colleague in the same organisation. He continued, "He is a master motivator as well as a mentor to the employees. I am just digging in. I like what I see around me, and I wish to make it big within the organisation. I am learning my ropes and I hope to rise to the position of the Sales Lead within the next few years."

"That is great to hear. So, hopefully, you have found your choice of career. I know you will do very well. I am so happy for you, and for us! Now tell me, what are you ordering for dinner? I would also like to have a pint of beer. I really want to try it. Will you order beer too or whiskey?"

"Guria, are you sure? A pint of beer? Who taught you all this?"

'Come on, Deepak! We are adults, and we can have fun sometimes. Although, I do not know whether we would end up having fun, having tried beer."

"So, adult girl, sorry, lady, allow me to order a drink for you and for myself. Do not go for beer directly. You might not like its taste. It is supposedly bitter."

"You are my man! Go ahead and order, please."

"Waiter, please get us a bottle of sparkling wine. Also get some finger food including some cheese balls. Thank you."

"Oh, wine and all, huh! You know a lot, it seems, about hard drinks."

'No, Guria. To be honest, I have heard stories from my friends about their dates. We have never done it ourselves because both of us were not into it. However, it has been a good week, and we can have this night to ourselves, to our shared lives, and to our shared future."

"You are a thorough gentleman, you know that? You keep amazing me with your simple but great attitude towards life. I do not wish to bug you here, but would you mind talking to Panditji or to your mother about us soon?"

"I wanted to speak to you about it, Guria. I plan to talk to my mother this week itself. Hopefully she would agree to help me speak to Panditji. Now that I am settled with a good job and a decent salary, I think they could allow me some liberty as an adult, to take my own decisions."

"You did not tell me about your salary, Deepak!"

"Have I ever asked you about your age, sweetheart? Never ask a man what his salary is." Deepak winked at Guria.

'Oh, okay, so you will not tell me about your salary. You are saying we have a shared future, but you do not want to tell me about such a trivial thing," Guria said, rather crossed.

"Just kidding, my love! I will get a monthly salary of six hundred rupees."

Guria broke into a laugh. "Oh, I was also kidding. I have complete faith in your abilities. You will do very well in your career, and you can foot some of our restaurant bills going ahead too!"

"Guria, the pleasure would be all mine."

"Listen, jokes aside, talk to your parents, get your house in order, and make me a part of your family. That is important. Till that time, you must keep saving enough for our future. Create a fixed deposit in a bank or, better still, create a recurring deposit."

"Yes, you are right. I also need to get a life insurance for myself, to secure our future even more."

"You are suddenly talking like my dad! Where is my sweet Deepak?"

"He is very much here." Deepak grinned as he took her hand into his own.

The waiter arrived with their order and poured the wine into two thin curved glasses.

"Cheers!" Deepak said, raising his glass.

"Cheers! This is to your job!" Guria crooned.

"To my job and to our life together," Deepak corrected her.

"To your job and to our life together!" Guria repeated.

It was a lovely evening with soft music playing in the background. The waiter had switched off the lights in the bar by then and kept candles on every table. The mood of the place suddenly shifted into a romantic setting.

Deepak and Guria enjoyed every bit of this togetherness. They loved the wine for its after-taste, and they also had a giddy feeling. They saw a few couples around them dancing slowly near the far end of the restaurant. It was the bar area, and by then they had a guitarist playing some foot-tapping music. Guria looked at Deepak longingly. He ignored her dance request as he felt like he was a non-dancer by birth. Guria got up and pulled him away and towards the dance floor. They went near the guitarist, and Guria started to slow dance around Deepak. Deepak was nonplussed, and stiff. Guria slowly touched his shoulders from behind, walked elegantly around him, caressed his cheeks, took his arms around her, and danced slowly to the beats. Deepak wished it were not happening to him, but he had no alternative. He went with the flow, and though he was not a dancer, he could see Guria glide around him, using him as a prop, dancing fluidly like a diva. He felt an ache in his heart, a longing to get near her. The feeling was so complete, he forgot about the people around him and he slowly kissed her on her lips. Guria kissed him back, softly but with passion. Their hearts melted, their tongues touched each other, and they passionately hugged each other. Guria sashayed around him, kissing him and touching him all over, quicker with a fastening pace of music. Deepak was taken that evening, and they had their first lip kiss, unlike they had ever thought before. It was love and lust both, in a potent mix. Guria asked him if he wanted to take her somewhere that evening, before getting back. Deepak considered it for a moment and reminded her of her own pledge not to do something stupid. She agreed. They had a great time, dancing and dining, laughing and cajoling, kissing and petting each other before Deepak dropped Guria home.

Chitra was disturbed seeing her daughter as it was very late into to the night, by the Patna standards. She also understood that Guria had consumed alcohol and guided her to her bedroom. She decided that she needed to have to have a chat with Guria soon.

She knew that Guria was a mature girl, but it was time they talked seriously. Chitra had heard only good things about Deepak till then, and she wanted to know more about him, not only from Guria but also from Rajendra. She hoped her daughter was with a guy who would take care of her, and truly love her. She wanted to make sure he was not pursuing her only for her looks. She hoped he wanted her for life, and wasn't playing around. She hoped he came from a good family background as well. She was tensed because of her husband's job sometimes, as they had seen some reverses in the business too. She hoped they would come out of all troubles, as a family, soon.

Chapter 13

1974

"Amit, please come along. It is going to be a silent rally by students from the various colleges of Bihar. Almost ten thousand students are going to be a part of it," Nakul said.

Nakul was Amit Agarwal's classmate, and they were just out of their teenage years.

"Okay, I will join the rally. I agree with JP's call for a peaceful rally. Students must make their presence felt in a democracy. Great changes can happen through student movements." Amit looked excited and full of conviction. He was inspired by the movies on the fight for the Indian independence. He continued, "By organising a massive but peaceful rally, one can achieve great strength and momentum in a movement that is pro-democracy, and against an autocratic regime."

"Let us then move towards the originating site quickly. The rally would commence anytime soon."

"Yes, let's go there. Look, they are tying every student's hand and gagging their mouths with a cloth. What an electric atmosphere! This is the power of democracy."

"You two, come here and get in this queue. You guys are late. Come, let me tie your hands, and listen, we are a part of a peaceful protest. We are against the rising prices and corruption. We are against the inappropriate use of our constitution by bringing in various uncalled for amendments. We are against this newly formed idea of India in the present times. We represent the Gandhian forces, and our leader is JP himself. We are blessed to have him handle various such protests and give a direction to the youth. We are pro-democracy, and we want an India that is great again. An India where no one sleeps hungry. An India where everybody has a roof over their heads. An India where there are no deaths due to starvation. And an India, where no farmer dies under the pressure of loan sharks. We are against all that is wrong, and JP would change it for the better. We are for a better future for our brethren. Come, join the rally, and protest this corrupt regime. Always remember, this is a peaceful rally. We do not think the police would use force to stop us. If, however, they do use force, we must stay and lie low," one of the organisers gave a long monologue to Amit and Nakul.

Both were happy to be a part of a historic rally. They were filed in a line soon. It was a massive show of strength. The rally meandered through the lanes and by-lanes and reached its destination peacefully. There was change in the air. This could lead to a bigger movement towards seeking a dissolution of the Bihar Assembly.

Amit went back home with a glint in his eyes. He was happy to have contributed to the national cause. He felt that it was only a matter of time the protests would have an effect on the central government, and they would be free of a tyrannical rule. He knew such protests worked magic with the commoners, and the momentum grew quickly. Youth had the energy and vitality to take the fight to the centre, and they had an able leadership at the state level, i.e. JP, to ensure the right approach. Those were heady days of a fledgling democratic fabric of India. The state had usurped all powers and the democratic institutions were at its mercy. People could not talk about the condition of their nation freely, else they invited the wrath of the mighty state machinery, and under MISA, their powers were absolute.

It was only through peaceful protests and through passing relevant and valid information, the Opposition could sustain its efforts for a dissolution of the parliament, and consequent elections. The nation's youth had an important role to play, which Nakul and Amit realised, as they rose up to the occasion that day.

Chapter 14
1973

"Good morning, or should I say, good afternoon? How is your head? Is it still spinning or aching?" Chitra asked Guria, with sarcasm in her tone.

'No, Mumma, I feel alright. I'm sorry, I had wine yesterday evening during my celebrations with Deepak. Neither he nor I had tried it ever before, but we felt that it was okay to indulge a little bit, as it was a happy day for us." Chitra admonished Guria, gave her a loving slap on her face, and nodded at Guria to continue. Guria said, "Also, Mumma, Deepak was all praise for Babu. He said that the way Mr. Agarwal manages his employees is exemplary, and that he commands the respect of his entire staff. Deepak is very happy to have gotten the opportunity to work under Babu."

"Guria, your Babu was also telling me about it yesterday evening. He also likes Deepak and feels that he has a long and successful career ahead of him. He is hard-working and effective in his work, and he has the hunger to grow. He will go places. However, let me be very clear, once and for all; no more drinks till you are married. It is not there in our culture. What you do post-marriage is for your in-laws and your husband to decide. But while you are with us, you cannot drink. I did not tell your Babu about it, and neither will I ever do so. You know that he doesn't like drinking and has never partaken alcohol himself, even though, for his business, he attends parties where there's alcohol. I hope I am clear."

"Yes, Mumma, crystal. Please serve me some light food. I do not wish to eat much. As it is, I feel a bit heady."

Guria slowly munched on the *dosa* that her mother served and thought fondly about the previous evening. Her love for Deepak knew no bounds. She wanted to feel him, wanted to love him, and caress him. But then she felt shy, almost embarrassed, at her own thoughts. Her friends had asked her about the same, and had made fun of her. But Guria was not ready for any physical relations before marriage. The only thing she had taken a liberty in and had gone against the so-called social norms was choosing her life-partner herself, instead of waiting for her parents to do so, as it happened in arranged marriages in India.

She knew that Deepak was in it for the long run and that he was of a strong character. She was aware of his likes and dislikes and knew that he was happy in their relationship and did not ever wish to change the equation by introducing an element of pre-marital sex. They were content and they were in love. The only concern they had was whether they would be able to get married with the blessings from his parents.

"What's up, *di*? I heard you were drunk yesterday! Don't worry, mom didn't tell me. I just overheard you guys," Amit said, teasing Guria.

"Amit, please, don't tell Babu about it. This was my first and last time, I promise."

"Don't worry, di. I'm not going to tell him anything." Amit smirked, and Guria hit him on his back affectionately. They giggled together and broke into a jig. Amit then put on a serious face and said, "Anyway, are you aware of what's happening in the world besides your lovey-dovey life? Things are getting worse out there. A lot of decisions that the central government is taking do not bode well for our country. Our Prime Minister is going against the way our forefathers thought we would be governed."

"I know you read a lot of newspapers, but I don't like reading so much about current affairs. I am more into novels. However, you can speak to me about the ills of our times if you want to. I might be able to learn from you and understand your frustrations about the current situation of our country," Guria said like an elder sister would, supporting her brother. Then she added, "Babu also stays worried these days. Just the other day he was mentioning about the prices of all agricultural products going completely north."

"I know, didi. Our Prime Minister came to power on the promise of *Garibi Hatao*. She has a socialist bent of mind, and ordered the nationalisation of private banks in 1969." While Amit was passionately talking, Guria listened with utmost attention, showing serious concern on her face, enough for Amit to realise that she was playing with him. He reacted sharply, saying, "Didi, don't make fun of me, okay? And listen to me properly!" Amit made a cute face, as though he wanted something really important form his elder sister, and he had to break into that face to make her agree to his request. Guria laughed at this, caught Amit's nose and gave it a slight jerk. Amit removed her hand from his nose, and said in a more involved voice, "Thereafter, she has had confrontations with the Supreme Court on various matters. She abolished the Privy Purse. Later, she made two major amendments in the constitution so that the Judiciary could not stop her in the tracks. Eventually, she got a particular judge to supersede three other senior judges and become the Chief Justice of the Supreme Court. She has done it all with an agenda. She is just destroying the institutions of our country."

"I did not think you had political science as a subject, did you?" Guria said, pinching Amit's nose once again.

Chapter 15

1974

"Amit, you must not go to today's rally. I will tell Babu if you do. It is getting increasingly violent and there could be lathi charge and arrests by the police. Listen to me, please," Guria pleaded with her brother.

"Didi, I am not wearing any bangles."

"God, what are you even saying, Amit! How can you be a man who thinks women are weak? I thought better of you."

"Di, I would advise you not to take it personally. I know you are better than a lot of men in your work and otherwise too. In any case, I did not mean it that way."

"I get it. You feel that you must contribute to the protests, and you should be a part of the history that is being written politically in our country today."

"Di, even that is not important. I wish to add to the numbers who are there with the opposition leaders today.

They wish to take this government to task, based only on the real facts."

"I am not against the protests, Amit. As your elder sister, I care for you, and I wish to see you safe."

"Di, no one is safe in our country today. Even if you do not take a part in the protests, you are not safe. Safety is a mirage, and we are just misled by the calm before the storm."

"Okay, I agree, but I want you safe and I will not allow you to go anywhere. Not to the rally, especially after knowing the dangers."

"Di, do not do this to me. I have always agreed to what you have asked of me, but allow me to join this rally. I will take care of myself."

"Amit, I implore you not to go there today. It might not be safe at all. I will tell Babu about it."

"Di, our economy is in the doldrums and the government is autocratic. They are using the baton to talk to the protestors. There is no political discourse in the country at present, other than what JP's next step would be." Saying thus, Amit took Guria's face in his palms, looked affectionately towards her, and kissed her temple. Guria hugged Amit in return, kissed him on his cheeks, and held his hand whispering that she did not want him to go. Amit felt torn apart, and Guria could see it on his face.

Amit said, "I am a committed student soldier of the movement, didi. I understand the gravity of the situation and will take utmost care to remain aloof for my own safety. I, however, wish to be there on the historic day. I request you to not to tell anything to Babu just yet. Please wait just a bit longer, just until I leave for the protest site."

Guria reluctantly agreed, but she had a bad feeling about it.

The government had converted the city into a fortress where normal intra-state buses or even the trains were not allowed to ply. They had also sealed all borders. Policing was going on at the *ghats* too. They even denied the boatmen entry to the ghats and were sailed back to Hajipur. Guria felt that there was a good chance of a massive police crackdown on the rally.

Meanwhile, after a couple of hours, Amit and Nakul reached the protest site, and saw the scene from a distance. Nakul wanted to go near the epicentre of the protest.

"Today is going to be bad, Nakul. It could turn violent, and so I think we should be at a good distance away from the centre of the protest."

"Don't worry. We will stand far from the main area of congregation. Did you hear today's stories?"

"No, I haven't. That's why I came here. Tell me the important ones." Nakul was perched on the boundary wall, for a better view. Amit also got up on the boundary and they could see the congregation nearby.

Nakul continued, "There is a massive police presence at all major checkpoints. They have turned people back on all bus routes. However, a lot of people have entered through various other ways. We have heard several dead bodies have come to Patna for cremation today."

"Dead bodies? Why is that significant? They normally come every day, don't they?"

"They do. But the numbers were over ten times of the normal today. It is said that these were the old people who wanted to attend the rally. As part of a dead bodies' march towards cremation centres, a decent crowd of people could sneak in. None of them were dead, but they were only following that protocol to squeeze into Patna." Nakul was animated in his description, and he enacted the part of a funeral procession. He was in his baggy pants and an oversized shirt. He was fair and short, but skeletal. He normally wore oversized clothes, as he felt that it gave an impression of decent health. He also wore glasses with a thick frame, something like the 70s movies. He had sidelocks that almost went to his chin on either side.

"Oh, that is quite innovative. Didn't the police realise their folly?"

"I guess they did not, else they would have started checking the dead bodies to check whether they were dead or not. Also, a lot of people sneaked in from Hajipur, travelling halfway by boats and the rest by swimming. The boats were being sent back, so a few of the more committed soldiers just swam." He took a mouthful of *paan masala* in his mouth. Amit thought that Nakul would be quiet for a moment, as his mouth was full. They could concentrate on the scene developing in front of them. He felt that it was a fight that JP would win. No matter what anyone did, public opinion could not be controlled and suppressed for long.

Nakul chewed hurriedly at the masala inside his mouth and spat a mouthful on the street beneath. He said, "Amit *yaar*, let's go a little further. There is no commotion here so far. This is a tense atmosphere. There is a large police presence, but they seem to be quite docile. Things don't seem to be turning violent anytime soon."

"Let's still maintain a safe distance. We should stay here. Yes, this is a good vantage point. The speakers have started their speeches. We must listen to them. This is a discourse in political science. This is how revolutions are planned and carried out. We must learn and implement them later, whenever required." They listened intently to the speech being given at that moment.

Then suddenly, there was a huge commotion. The police had opened water cannons and lathi charge in various areas to control and disperse the crowds. The Journalists were also getting beaten and their cameras were being taken away.

Amit and Nakul could hardly even understand what was happening when a policeman charged after them. They tried to run away but by the time they got off the boundary wall, the policeman hit Amit on the head with his baton. Nakul also got hit on his legs, and they both fell onto the ground. Amit was bleeding profusely from his head and an ambulance quickly carried him away, while Nakul was left there to fend for himself.

Nakul somehow managed to catch hold of a rickshaw and went straight to Amit's house.

"*Aunty ji*, Amit was badly hurt by a police baton. They have taken him away in an ambulance. They must have gone to a public hospital. I got hit in my leg too and can barely walk."

"Oh God! I kept telling him not to take part in such events. The police were after students more than anybody else, as this has been given form of a student's movement. Was there anyone to take care of Amit? Was there any doctor inside the ambulance?"

"I don't know, aunty. I am in tremendous pain myself, so couldn't see properly."

"You come inside. Let me send someone to inform Guria ke papa about it. He should go to the hospital as soon as possible."

"Oh Mumma, even I told him not to go. I told him that the state administration was ready for today's event and there would be violence. He told he would stay away from the central area of the protest," Guria said.

"Didi, we were indeed far away from the main protest area. But all of it started very suddenly. There was total chaos, they started water cannons and lathi charge, and we got hit out of nowhere by a lathi wielding policeman."

Chapter 16
1975

"Panditji is busy today with the planning. He might not get any time today to converse with us," the Shayar lamented.

"You are correct, Farooqui Saheb. There seems to be a massive upsurge in the arrests of political leaders today. We have not heard about the proclamation of the Emergency or the resignation of our Prime Minister though," the Professor twitched his moustache while speaking. He did not look comfortable. He expected an escalation in the governmental action against the protestors. He felt that the wind blew in the opposite direction, and that it could uproot many a twig on its path. It could take on formidable Opposition like JP too. He felt that it was time he counselled the people of his barrack to be vigilant. It was good to be silent and better still, all of them could vanish. Being in the prison when the country was going through a major political churn of the likes never seen before, in a free India, was dangerous.

Thoughtfully, he continued, "It is difficult to ascertain sitting here in prison as to what is happening outside. But this much is certain—the situation is grim and in a state of flux. Things have really taken a bad turn. It might be a pre-emptive move by the incoming Prime Minister to put most of the opposition members in prison, before assuming office."

Rajendra seemed to agree, and he nodded, saying, "That way, he/she would have no opposition in the term initially and the current situation could be handled deftly. That would still be okay. However, if the other alternative is true, that is, Emergency has been proclaimed, or is going to be proclaimed—it would be a very sad day for our country."

"I think there is a political will to proclaim Emergency. There wouldn't have been so many arrests otherwise," the Shayar added.

In the case of a normal resignation by the then honourable Prime Minister, the incoming Prime Minister would have taken the path of least resistance. It would be easy to explain and fight in the upcoming elections, had the serving Prime Minister resigned to respect the constitution of India. They could have then projected themselves as the saviours of democracy and demanded another chance. This, however, looked sinister. Something bad was at play. People expected the worst outcome of the showdown with the Judiciary and with the Opposition.

"*Yeh kis raah par le ja rahe ho humein, ae parvardigar,*
Jin galiyaron mein main bhatak raha hoon, thodi si tapish hai, aur thodi si baaki hai;
Rahein aasaan nahin magar kaanton par chal kar jaana hai,
Abhi abhi toh hindostan ka janam hua hai;
Yeh kahaan hamein dhakel rahe ho,
Ae khuda ke bandon;
Arzoo thi hamein ki ik farishta sa wazir-e-azam mile,
Bas jamhooriyat chalti rahe, Farooqui ki aisi guzaarish hai!"

(On which path are you leading us, my Lord,
There is some anguish still left in the lanes I wander;
The path isn't easy, but we must walk on thorns,
India was born only recently;
Where are you pushing us,
Oh, God's men;
We desired an angelic Prime Minister,
Just let democracy prevail, that's Farooqui's only request.)

"Awesome! You are good, Shayar. It comes naturally to you, doesn't it?" Rajendra asked.

"It's all God's grace, I'm myself insignificant. What is Farooqui's status to raise any complaints?" the Shayar replied.

"Guys, we are in for a shock. Can you see so many leaders being brought in today? Let's go to our barrack. I sense a lot of trouble going ahead." Saying this, the Professor rose to his feet and the others too got up to get back to their barrack.

A little while later, Panditji found the Professor in the barrack. He called him outside and told him something. The Professor's face went pale. Panditji advised him to go back and counsel everyone to be quiet. They should go about their normal routine but keep themselves away from any congregations. It was going to be a difficult night and they had to see it through as silently as possible.

The Professor got back into the barrack, and seeing his crestfallen expression, the others approached him.

"Friends, there's a terrible news. I would request your patience and discretion. Please follow the request and listen to the communication received just now. Let me first request all of you to maintain absolute silence. I do not want any one of you to shout or to create a scene over here." The Professor had droplets of sweat on his brow. He removed them and looked towards his fellow mates. People awaited some terrible news. It could be about the imposition of the Emergency. He continued, "We are under heavy police presence today and it will now continue. The police have been given an order to maintain total peace within the jail, and to deal with any disturbance with full force. They can lathi-charge upon the slightest hint of indiscretion from any one of you."

"Professor Saheb, we will maintain peace. Please tell us what has happened. What is going on outside?" someone from the crowd asked.

"I am pained to say that this morning at 12 am, the Indian government has proclaimed the Emergency." There was a cry of anguish in the cell and though it was muted, everyone heard it within themselves. The Professor paused for effect, adjusting his right leg a bit, keeping his right hand on the wall near him. He continued, "The announcement has come only in the short speech that was telecast a while back. The Prime Minister has requested people to respect the law and order."

People understood that the decision was taken to prevent the country from going lawless and to protect the institutions. While the commoners did not need to worry, the government would expect the citizenry to perform their duties and to keep away from any sort of political congregations. People knew that there were sweeping powers with the state machinery and the police would soon become like demi-gods. All the powers of the state would be with the central government, and effectively with the PM, and therefore with the central government, while the Legislature and the Judiciary would only have a limited role.

The Newspapers did not get printed in Delhi that morning, as there was a massive power cut in the area where most of the press printers are located. The common person knew civil liberties would be withdrawn, and the country would be under an autocratic administration. "The tallest leaders of the opposition parties were taken into custody. Let us wait for things to settle down. That would be all," the Professor summed up and the entire crew listened to him like students. They quietly went about their routine, leaving their destinies in the hands of their motherland. It was difficult to believe the country would see this stage, so soon in her life.

Chapter 17
1975

"A lot is happening politically. I guess, by now, most of the senior leaders of the opposition parties are under arrest, and our job has become difficult. We must keep the political prisoners safe and away from the other inmates." Panditji said, and turned his head to his right slowly, before shifting it towards left in a semi-circular fashion. He stepped forward with his arm circling in a bowling action, stepped back, and stepped forward again. He did it a couple of times, got a bit of sweat on his temple, and made a purring sound from his mouth. The Professor and the others ignored his strange behaviour. Panditji further added, "Simultaneously, the new political prisoners would not follow the rules of engagement. They have to be taught a lesson. It is just to maintain law and order within the precincts of our jails across the country. I sense a lot of unprovoked lathi charges happening on flimsy grounds.

We would try our best not to resort to any such means, till we get at least some cooperation from the new inmates."

"We did not come here just to stay put and not contribute, did we?" Rajendra asked.

"We have contributed to the cause of this agitation in our own little way. What else could we have done? We are not political leaders. We are common people who have just taken part in the agitation," the Professor said and looked kind heartedly towards the Shayar and Rajendra.

He looked back at Panditji, and said, "I know all of us have lost a lot, personally. Are you aware that Rajendra ji had a flourishing trade of agricultural goods? Whilst he is here, it is being managed by his daughter. She was casually involved in the business earlier. Of course, she has a credible professional team to help her handle the day-to-day affairs, but the genius of Rajendra ji is missing from their business. They are just about doing okay." The Professor said, and pushed his hair backwards, adjusting it before perching his spectacles on the nose. Rajendra and the Shayar looked on, towards the Professor and towards Panditji. Rajendra felt a bit weak with the thought of the losses in his business and that his daughter had to work so hard to keep it running. The Professor continued, "Panditji, Rajendra ji has lost a lot of business to his rivals. He would have to mend the situation once he gets back."

Rajendra looked a bit aloof, with his head down, thinking about his personal contribution as a common citizen of the country, to a cause he believed was vital for the well-being of the people. The Professor said, "Also, you might not be aware that he has a young son as well. He was just nineteen when he took part in the protest on the 6th of October. He wanted to see the top leaders give speeches on stage and guide the crowd towards *Swarajya*."

"What about him?" Panditji interjected inquisitively. The Professor continued, a little unnerved by the interjection, but taking it in stride, "Do you know what happened to him? He was chased by a policeman, even though he was far away from the epicentre of trouble. He got hit on his head by a lathi and became disabled for life. He is on a wheelchair now, but he goes to the office with his elder sister and helps her with accounting. He has given a lot to this agitation already, and the very fact that he is here with us is difficult to digest. Democracy comes at a heavy personal price. We see it ourselves today. We need to keep it, rather, we need to win it back!" The Professor said, with a sense of urgency.

"Oh, I'm sorry to hear that, Rajendra ji! But can I ask you something? Does a boy by name Deepak work in your firm? He is a youngster who joined last year." Panditji questioned.

"Yes, but how do you know Deepak?" Rajendra was surprised.

Panditji rounded his hands in his typical style over his belly, had a big smile on his large and roundish face, adjusted his big frames on his nose, and said, "He is Deepak Pandit, my eldest son. Oh, so now I realise you are the gentleman who gave my son a job in his tough times. He was about to go to Delhi, but his planetary positions were not good, and he was advised against it. That is when through a solid reference, he interviewed and was immediately given a job at your large trading firm."

"That is not fully true. He is a great guy and an admirable professional. He is also a very quick learner. In fact, my daughter, Guria is being helped by him. He has been helping her with client management and new sales leads. He is a committed soldier and a good man. I am surprised that we have met so many times, but we got to know things about one another this way. Our lives have been intertwined. Anyway, coming back to Deepak, you are a proud father!" Rajendra remarked.

"I have heard something else as well. I think Deepak loves Guria and they wish to get married. Deepak has had a couple of talks on the issue with my wife, but they have not brought it up with me yet. I think they are afraid I would say no to the proposal." Panditji took a high ground position, and spoke with a slightly changed but strong and deep voice, "They are correct in thinking so as our castes are different. I am a firm believer in the caste system as propagated by our forefathers. We should continue the system and bless it so that it continues well into the future. That is the only thing which has saved India till now." While he spoke, the Professor looked towards Panditji with a slight disgust, and then at Rajendra, and at the Shayar. The Shayar and Rajendra got the twist. However, Panditji continued in his strange manner, "We can see that marriage as an institution has crumbled worldwide. Here in India too, it has started to crumble in the larger cities.

With love marriage and things like that happening, we are also going towards a fail-safe way of digging the grave of our cultural and societal well-being."

"You are passionate about the caste system, I see," Rajendra observed.

"Yes, I am. And I am sorry, but you should also be," Panditji retorted.

"I do believe in the institution of marriage, love or arranged. In this case, however, I have a feeling that this would turn out to be more of an arranged marriage," The Professor blurted out.

The others looked at him inquisitively, so he explained further, "Look, your son and his daughter have been meeting for at least two years or more. Now, tell me, have they taken any hasty step? Your son has not even come with his proposal to you yet, and he is trying to negotiate with his mom for the same. He respects you. He is willing to wait to get his love. He is a great guy!" He looked intently at Panditji, with a confidence Panditji knew this man of knowledge possessed. Panditji was all ears, as were Rajendra and the Shayar.

"On the other hand, your daughter has also been waiting for him to do so, out of her love for him and out of her respect for the elders. Such marriages must be blessed by us elders. They have not eloped, and that is surprising because it is a common occurrence. Change your prisms and look at it differently. They must live their lives, much beyond ours. They are in a committed relationship. However, they are waiting for their respective parents to bless them. They have seen difficult times and they have continued to wait. Do you have only one son, Panditji?" The Professor enquired.

"I have two sons—Deepak and Kul. I have a lot of expectations from Deepak. Kul is different anyways and if he loves someone, he will marry her, irrespective of what anyone thinks or says!"

"So, you are punishing your elder son because he happens to respect you and listen to you? If you cannot control your younger son, you do not have any reason to control your elder son in this matter either." The Professor was at his debating best and continued, "I see it thus, and I would say it loud and clear—you must agree to the marriage and have a happy family. I know that Deepak and Guria would continue to respect your authority and they would give you a wonderful old age. You would have good grandkids. Do not destroy their lives, because of your own notions. We are a generation or two above them and the times are changing. This reminds me, Rajendra ji. Are you okay with them getting married?"

"Well, I blessed them as soon as I got to know about my daughter's love. I learned that Deepak was a good guy from a genuinely nice family and background. For me, my daughter's life and her happiness are way too important. I cannot see her not get married to Deepak. They are deeply in love, and have kept away from each other till now, only as a mark of respect for both the family's bonds." Rajendra had sweat all over his face by then, and he gulped a glass of water, before continuing, "They could not go earlier to

Panditji as we had such a big disaster in our family, with the big blow that my son Amit took in his life. We are a very loving family and Guria was devastated. My kids are now clutching at straws to get their lives back, while I am here with you guys. Thank you, Professor Saheb, for your explanation of family ties and bonds."

"So, you agreed to their marriage, Rajendra ji? You do not believe in marriage within the same community, do you?" Panditji asked.

"I had till now believed in marriage within the same community and within the same sub-groups and castes. However, for me, my kids are more important than upholding the values of the caste system, which has not given its due to anyone, I guess." He got up, moved a step or two, and got back on his seat, before saying passionately, "It is an archaic system, which was created only to secure certain jobs for certain types of people, and it should have been long dead in a modern society. That we continue to hold on to it says that we have not evolved as a society."

"I also love my sons, as much as you love your kids. But that should not take away our responsibilities to the society," Panditji countered.

"I want to say something for your sake. Today, I don't feel like reciting poetry, or else, I'd have said it in a different way. Would you give this humble guy a little time to speak? The Shayar asked Panditji.

"Yes, please go ahead, sir!"

"I have a small request. I want to tell you that all of you have God's blessings in the form of your children. You ask me. I didn't have any offspring. If I had, then perhaps I too would not have understood their importance. Be thankful to God that you have children and just be a good father to them. Nothing else matters," the Shayar said calmly, although his voice was laced with a deep unspoken emotion of his heart.

"Oh, you are so right, Farooqui saheb! I wholeheartedly agree with you that kids are God's blessings, and we, as parents, must look after their happiness and well-being. Nothing else is of any importance," the Professor concurred.

"Empathy, my friend, empathy. That is what makes us, well, humans. Look at Professor saheb. He has two little kids, now possibly five and three. He was in Simdega when he was arrested and brought here. He had counselled his wife, who was alone with the kids, to take care of them and go to their larger family at Ranchi," Rajendra said, and looked around for some support, and seeing the Shayar nod at him, he continued further, "She must have faced quite a lot of issues. Can you imagine giving up one's job and family to come here for a cause you believe in? He was a very good teacher, and he was at his professional best, when he gave it all up. Upon news that he had been arrested and was being taken to Patna via Ranchi, the entire bus stand had welled up with students, teachers, and other common citizens who were not, in any way, involved in our fight." Rajendra patted the Professor on his back, giving him a side-hug, and then said, "He was a big guy, you see, and now he might not be able to go back to his college or to any other college ever again. He has taken that call and is living with it. He listened carefully to his conscience, and he took such a grave call. It was obviously painful for him and for his entire family."

Rajendra continued, "Well, let me tell you, Panditji. I had told my daughter that the day she wanted, I would go to your house and keep my *pagdi* at your feet. I would have requested you to allow their marriage, even if it meant having to take any form of insult. I am happy, however, that our kids are mature, and they said that they would sort it out themselves over time and would come to us only for our blessings." He had a tear in his eye, wiped it, and said, "Let me also tell you, Panditji, that your son did not know that I was his future father-in-law. My daughter never mentioned that to him, because had she done so, being the upright person that he is, he would not have joined our firm. He came to know that much later, after the tragedy with my son." Rajendra got up from the discussion table and went towards his barrack.

"Oh, the discussion got a bit heated up! Panditji, we would request you to think about all that we had to say. You would do a great service to yourself and to your wife. Also, there is no doubt that you would go multiple notches up in the eyes of your kids. It takes courage to do the right thing. Walk that extra step and take that decision. The world is yours!" The Professor said and he also got up.

The meeting was over. Panditji walked towards his office mulling over the importance of all the discussion that had just transpired. The father's love in him wanted to bless his son and get him married to Guria. But the Pandit in him stopped him short and counselled him to think better.

He decided to have a chat with Anjana and then take a call later. The times were not ripe anyways and he was under tremendous strain at work. Everything would have to be thought thoroughly, carefully dissected with reasoning and the implications. And it could happen some other day. Today, he needed to keep the jail peaceful and all the inmates safe.

Chapter 18

1975

Guria took the day off from the office. She had no clue what she was doing with her life. She could not see a resolution happening to her marriage issue with Deepak, as Deepak had not spoken to his father yet. Guria's father was in prison, and they had to wait it out. Deepak did not wish to speak to his father till his would-be father-in-law was in prison, even if for a laudable cause. Deepak knew his father would never be comfortable with an in-law in jail. The fate of the country was taking a turn for the worse, and she was worried.

The only consolation was that Deepak had spoken to his mother, who had heard him out without telling him about her opinion on the subject. She had kept her feelings to herself, knowing fully well that her words in the absence of a conversation with her husband would be useless. Guria knew that it was difficult for Anjana to commit to her son about their marriage. Panditji was known to have deep issues with marriage outside their caste, and unless he saw a new perspective, he would be dead against any such union.

Guria was deeply invested in Deepak, but it would come to naught if Panditji did not agree to their union. She got uncomfortable, the more she thought about her position. She wished to be with Deepak all her life, but she knew she had to move on if the marriage was not approved by Panditji. Guria's parents, Rajendra and Chitra were okay with her decision either way, and Rajendra had committed to her to meet Panditji and ask him for his son's hand, if and when Guria felt the time was ripe.

Guria knew even that may not be enough if Deepak did not take a stand. She did not think Deepak would ever take a stand against his father's wishes. She believed in a proverb all her life, "When the going gets tough, the tough get going." She believed she was tough, and she was made of sterner stuff. She would swing the decision in their favour, and she mulled over her options. She did not wish to speak on the same to Deepak as she had done so on many occasions in the past, and she knew speaking to him on this matter might only add bitterness to their relationship. She decided to speak to her mother soon. Her father was in the prison in Patna, and talking to him at the moment was not helpful. She felt helpless and distressed at the thought of her father in prison, she was worried about his food intake and his health. She felt so in need of a magic wand that could correct her situation at the drop of a hat.

Guria was sitting in a park near the state secretariat, alone, pensive and morose. She knew she needed to push her way through as she truly loved Deepak and she wanted to be with him, all her life.

She remembered how their relationship blossomed like a flower slowly opening its petals to the sun rays. They had been in a six-month dating period. She had to take the lead in telling Deepak how she felt about him and their relationship. Deepak was a good boy, but he was slightly timid for his age and for her liking. However, she knew that he was from a good family background, and he was innocent. She knew he was one of the few in their college, who did not actively seek relationships or even one-night stands. She also believed that he was a virgin as in her own relationship with him, he took the least interest in moving towards any form of a proper physical contact. What made matters worse for them was that he was terrorised of the prying eyes around them. He was genuinely considerate towards girls, but he kept aloof.

Guria knew even back then, that it was difficult to get such boys in these times. So, she decided to fight any battle to have him. She knew the battle had begun a long time back for her, but he was only getting ready, probably, to confront Panditji on his archaic views.

She looked at the beauty all around her in the different fragrances of flowers. She allowed herself to sink deeper into herself, motivate herself for the battle ahead, and dig deeper for any answers that her mind asked. She had a deep-seated worry, but she knew that she had to take the fight and win her life back for herself. She knew that at least her family was supportive, and they would do all in their power to see her happy.

The evening breeze blew slowly carrying the scent of her being. She was one with nature at that hour, and felt relaxed. She loved her own kitchen garden, and knew a bit about plants and flowers. She knew how to take care of them, and she felt happy in their company. Nature was her last resort when she felt disturbed, or in pain, and whenever she had unanswered questions in her life. She knew nature would find answers for her and she had faith in the Almighty. She knew that He would take care of her.

She knew that Deepak was worried for her, while he was in office, and she was here. Deepak was on the way to pick her up and take her home. They might probably go for a quick coffee before heading home. She did not expect much from life, but she knew that she had a fight ahead and she was prepared for it, better than ever in the past.

Chapter 19
1975

"Anjana, can we sit in the veranda, please? Ask someone to get a cup of coffee for me. Where are the kids?" Panditji asked his wife, slowly sitting on the garden chair in the veranda. There were only two chairs in the veranda, with a small cane glass centre table, and a few flowerpots having lush green leaves with only a couple of buds. The veranda had hanging plants providing foliage to parched souls during the summer season. Sunlight filtered through the foliage in a rhythmic fashion, creating its own little play of lights. Panditji liked sitting there for a bit after his office, as it provided him a source to connecting with nature and with Anjana, who was his strength and his companion for life.

The veranda overlooked their small compound, and it faced the road. Panditji did not mind the horns and the road noises. He felt relaxed while sitting there, in his own garden of life. It was important for him to be with family, and he felt relaxed. He observed that the paint in his house had started to peel off and it needed repainting. It was a costly affair and Panditji had kept it for some time in the future, like when he would get his elder son married. Only he did not know when that time would come in their lives.

He could smell *pakoras* being fried in the neighbouring flat, and he felt like having one himself as well. By that time Anjana came and she understood his mind. They were friends first in their relationship and spouses later, but not in the traditional sense of having met that way pre-marriage. Theirs was an arranged marriage, through the *gauna* route, but they became good friends in their marriage. Between the two of them, they were completely transparent, and they understood each other well.

"Deepak would be back from work after an hour. Kul has gone to a friend's place for some group project work. Give me a couple of minutes, I'll join you." Anjana went back to the kitchen and soon enough Panditji realised she was also frying pakoras. It fired up his belly in a way no breads could, and no cakes could ever imagine.

Panditji was busy reading the day's newspaper, when Anjana came in with his coffee, and a cup of tea for herself.

"Thanks. Sit here," Panditji said, pulling a chair close to himself.

"What's the matter, Panditji? I hope everything's okay. Have you put in your papers at work?"

"No, no, there is nothing like that. Can we not just sit and have a cup of coffee together?"

"No, we can't. Don't you see you are the only one having coffee here?" Anjana made a mocking face and laughed. Panditji had a broad smile on his face, and he felt relaxed. His face beamed and he felt energetic. Anjana saw him and egged him further, saying, "Seems like...you have found a lover after all. You look different today, happy and content. It also seems like you will ditch me soon."

"I'm not so good at making small talk. But it is not what you think. It is better, I guess. Okay, so here it is. I wanted to speak to you about something important," he said and paused briefly, looked away for a moment thoughtfully, and continued, "You have still not told me anything about Deepak and his girlfriend. I am aware of it. In fact, I have been meeting her father time and again and we have become very good friends."

"Oh, that is surprising! What kind of a person is he?" Anjana asked.

"He is a genuinely good person and a self-made businessman. I was not aware that he is Guria's father. He is a prisoner in my own jail."

"Then how can he be a good person?"

"Don't worry about that. He has not committed any crime. He is in jail only because he is a political prisoner, just like JP."

"Oh, I get it. So, when did you get to know?"

"Recently, and in quite a dramatic manner during a conversation. There are these three friends I have inside the jail. One of them is a professor, the other is a Shayar, and the third one is a businessman i.e. Guria's father. So, we suddenly got to know that Deepak works in his company and that Guria is his daughter." Panditji drank another sip of coffee, looked at Anjana, who had, by then, left her cup on the table, and said, "His son, Amit, was hit on the head by a policeman on the 6th of October during the large rally in Patna and he is maimed for life. So, we eventually spoke about Deepak and Guria and all of them wanted the two to be married while I held on to my beliefs of the caste system. However, what the Shayar said, has hit me hard."

"What did he say?" Anjana asked inquisitively. She saw a soft expression on Panditji's face, and she could guess the story was taking a positive turn.

"Well, he doesn't have any kids and he is greatly pained because of that. He said that our kids are like blessings, and we need to keep them happy and safe." Panditji looked at Anjana. She knew that it was a moment of truth for him, and for them as a family. Would they be bound by what they thought was best for their kids, or should they listen to others with an open mind? Panditji continued, "He said that we must take care of them and go beyond our beliefs and agree to do all that would eventually turn out to be good for them. Ever since then, I have been thinking about Deepak. He is a genuinely good boy. He has not come to me yet, although they have been thinking of marriage for over two years now. His silence is now killing me."

Anjana took a cue from Panditji's words and thoughtfully said, "All we wanted was a girl from our caste. If that is not something that the Gods would give us, so be it. If you are okay, we should speak to Deepak.

Ask him to speak to Guria and arrange a meeting with her parents. Are you saying this? But you also said her father was in your prison."

"Yes, but I did not tell you that they are being released tomorrow. It was God's wish that he became such a good friend of mine. It was God's wish that he became a prisoner in my prison in the first place. It is also God's wish that Deepak should marry Guria. So please, set it up," he felt relieved as a they took a major decision that would change the lives of their offspring. They knew that it was the best decision for him.

"You know, I'm so happy today! Deepak was correct."

"Why do you say so? What did he tell you that you have kept from me?"

"He always said that you would come around. You would see the pain in his eyes and would agree to this marriage."

"But neither of you guys ever asked me about this marriage. How I understood is a separate matter."

"Aren't you intelligent?"

"If you say so," saying thus, Panditji held Anjana in his arms. She flushed and moved him away from her.

"Oh, Deepak will be so thrilled. You have surprised me today, and I suddenly realise that our son would get married. He has grown big!"

"Yes Anjana. Our son is now of a marriageable age and hopefully he is mature enough to handle it. Look, Guria is from a very good family background. He needs to treat her well."

"He is quite mature for his age and he loves Guria to the moon. I would be least worried on that count."

"Super. So, I would invite the other two friends of mine with their families too. The Shayar will come as he is from Patna only. However, I guess it would be difficult for the Professor. He would return to Ranchi after his release. He will have to find a job for himself, all over again. May God be with him!"

"I will serve *kheer* after dinner today. Let me go and prepare it. Today is such a happy day!" Anjana exclaimed and ran towards kitchen. She was joyous as Panditji.

He felt relieved that his friends had shown him the right direction, else, he would have pushed Deepak in a manner that would have been devastating for Deepak and for Guria. He knew that sometimes our kids show us a better path and we should go with the flow. We should seek a wider counsel and agree to change ourselves when required.

That was a day when Panditji had taken a sensible decision for everyone—but Kul, Deepak, or Guria's family had no clue yet.

Chapter 20
1975

"So, that's it? Why are they releasing us today? They would have liked to keep us here, wouldn't they?" Rajendra asked Panditji.

"While you guys have been here for a couple of months, under preventive detention, the leaders of the agitation were outside and taking the cause forward. Now, it is their turn to serve time in prisons all over the country," Panditji said in a reconciliatory tone, half-happy for the political prisoners who were in preventive custody. He knew that all the leaders from the opposition parties would soon be incarcerated and there would be no place left in prisons for anyone who was there in preventive custody.

The orders from the top bosses were clear. They wished to quickly prepare the prisons for the opposition leaders and retain only the other criminals. The police were ordered to release everyone else. It was a talk of the town that the government officers were directed to be on time in their offices. Trains were to ply on time, and everyone had to work. The times were changing. While the productivity of the government would improve with an autocratic style of governance, the country had to witness its ills, sooner than later.

Panditji counselled his three friends, "Keep away from rallies and protests, for you would feel an iron-hand come down. Moreover, you must go to your homes and get started with your lives. You have achieved quite a bit for the country, have you not? It was a fight to the finish and the government had an upper hand initially, as it always happens, with brute power in their hands. However, in a democracy, even during the suspension of the same for a while, people should get together and fight the oppression with a force that hasn't been seen before."

Panditji also told them, "There is absolutely no disturbance anywhere and peace is being maintained at the point of a gun. People are supposed to perform their duties and not talk about politics."

There was another change that was happening at a brisk pace. It seemed to the masses that the honourable Prime Minister's younger son was assuming a lot of power in the government. He had become very powerful while the cabinet had been reduced to a rubber stamp.

"Yes, I would go back to Ranchi and try and get a job or something. I could even start a coaching centre. At least, I would be with my family, and they would be very happy to have me back. The kids miss me a lot, you know. And I miss them too," The Professor said, a tad emotionally. "I do not remember whether I recounted to you how I was held. This happened despite warnings from my fraternity, my father and above all, my life-partner," The Professor asked.

"That's something none of us have told the another about ourselves. I am surprised how," Rajendra thoughtfully answered.

"Well, in my case it was a given. I did not listen to people around me, who counselled against my continuous rants against the state policy. I spoke out loud in front of my students in classes, in our staff room, in front of the elite of the society in my small town. Word of course spread and a few people, including my principal told me to be careful and to be a mute spectator to the goings-on in the country. My wisdom told me otherwise. I have no regrets, though. I did what I could for my country."

Rajendra then said, "My story was rather simple. It was decided by the seniors in their industry that every family should have at least one son in the silent march. I decided against sending his daughter there, so I had to be there instead to show faith in the silent movement against tyranny and oppression by government of the day. I was unlucky, as with my burly tummy I moved slowly during the police crackdown. So, I surrendered."

Everyone looked at the Shayar now. The Shayar was active in the community meetings, and he was a face of many rallies. These were more of religious rallies and meetings, but he was seen by the policemen on multiple occasions. So at least in the case of the Professor and the Shayar, they were aware of the consequences, and they wanted to be a part of the agitation against the government in some measure. For Rajendra though, it was a single event-outing.

Rajendra said, "Your family would be waiting for you. However, I would request you to come with me to my house. You could spend just this night with us and leave by tomorrow night's train. That would give both me and my family a lot of happiness. You are a great friend, after all."

"That would be fantastic! I would love to come over and meet your wife and your kids," the Professor said with a beaming smile. They looked at each other and hugged. Thereafter, Panditji looked towards the professor, the Shayar and Rajendra. He took the Shayar in his arms and hugged him.

"*Apna bahum bus itna hi tha,*
Aisa kyun mukaddar hai;
Hum garamjoshi se milte rahenge,
Aisi ik khwahish hai!"

(Our togetherness was only till this point,
Why is destiny like this;
I have a single wish,
That we keep meeting with the same fervour!)

As soon as the Shayar said these words, the others hugged him and one another. They wished not to part, but life was calling them back. The Jailor, Panditji was also sad at their departure. He had gotten used to spending a good amount of time every day with them and drinking their morning cup of tea together. That routine was now going to change, possibly for the worse, going ahead.

While professor saheb left with Rajendra, the Shayar left for his own home. Panditji too returned home as he was not feeling quite well. Anjana was a little alarmed to see Panditji's condition and she immediately got him into bed and made him some fresh vegetable soup.

"How are you feeling now? What's the matter? I have seldom seen you back home in the afternoon. Do you need any medicine?" Anjana asked, sitting beside him.

"No, I'm just... a little down. But the soup has made me feel better. My friends were released today. The Professor went to Rajendra's house for a day, and he'll return to Ranchi by tomorrow evening's train. I was wondering if I could call my friends and their better halves home tonight. What do you say?" Just the two couples and the Professor."

I doubt if Rajendra ji would come to our place right now. I have not spoken to Deepak about our talk yesterday, and they are not aware that you are okay with his marriage to Guria. Would you like to announce it today? Would you seek Rajendra ji and his wife's approval for Deepak's marriage with Guria? What's your plan?" Anjana enquired.

"Let me invite them fist, Anjana. They will all come over, of that I have full confidence. They are my best friends. I will not tell him anything about Guria and Deepak over the phone," Panditji said with a slight smirk. He continued, "We will take it as it comes tonight. I have high hopes in my friends, and I presume that the evening will turn out for good. I hope you will be able to manage with all the dinner arrangements."

"Yes, I will manage it. Don't worry. You call them over."

Chapter 21
1975

"Anjana, I have sent my car to pick up the Shayar and his wife, *Begum* Najma ji. Rajendra ji and Professor saheb have confirmed that they would be arriving here in a short while. Chitra ji, the better half of Rajendra ji, is also coming."

"You are not allowed to call her "begum" Najma. She is only the Shayar's begum. Your friendship does not give you any rights over his begum!" Anjana said, with a loud laugh. Panditji loved Anjana's carefree attitude. She was a happy person intrinsically, and her laughter was magical. It would induce a smile to his face, instantaneously. She also knew he would only briefly smile at things that made her have a hearty laugh.

"Oh yes, my bad! She is Farooqui's begum! I have my begum here in front of me," Panditji grinned.

"I am so glad you have called them over, especially Rajendra ji and Chitra ji." She looked at Panditji and smiled. Panditji asked her if she told Deepak anything about their previous day's conversation. Anjana told him she had not, and in fact she had asked Deepak to get home a bit later in the evening, more towards 9 pm. He was inquisitive about it, but he also said in any case he would be late. He had an important meeting and has gone to Patna City. Panditji was glad she had not foretold anything to Deepak.

"I think he knows about the entire program through Guria by now," Panditji thoughtfully said, continuing, "It is very difficult to keep any surprises nowadays. In our days, little things could surprise us. Do you remember one evening when *pujya pitaji* and *mataji* had gone to take a stroll?" Anjana flushed, and she pushed Panditji aside, moving towards the kitchen. "Leave me alone for some time. I have a lot of work to do. You have called so many people, including my son's to-be in-laws. Go get some fruits and sweets. Panditji pulled her near him and again asked her if she remembered that evening. She tried to deflect him again, but Panditji held her and said, "I came home early to find you all decked up and I was thoroughly surprised. You made coffee for me that evening and we sipped it together, hand in hand, in our veranda. That is one evening I simply cannot forget, and that is the reason why I wish to have that kind of evening again and again, any time I am home early."

"Then you should be back home early more often," Anjana teasingly said, and went to change. She wanted to look her best for the evening, especially since her son's future in-laws were coming.

The gate keeper brought the Professor, Rajendra ji, and Chitra ji inside the living room. Panditji got up and welcomed them with open arms. The men shook hands and hugged one another while Panditji said *namaskar* to Chitra and ushered them all to sit down on the sofa. Anjana soon came out of the bedroom and joined them. She sat next to Chitra.

The evening began in high spirits, and the mood only got brighter when the Shayar also came in with his wife.

Panditji was hyper-active, taking care of the guests and their requirements while Anjana was shuttling between the kitchen and the living room, when Kul came home and was introduced to everyone. The Professor got him to have a seat next to him and engaged him in a chat, trying to figure out his intellect and his goals. He was happy to meet the young man. He had been away from his students for a long time, and he felt happy to have met a young ambitious boy.

A little later, at around nine, Deepak walked in and was rather surprised to see Rajendra ji at his home.

'Sir, when were you released from prison? Guria did not mention anything to me. But then, I did not go to the office today and neither could I call her as it was a very busy day. I was in Patna city, trying to finalise a trade deal."

"Deepak, so finally we can surprise you! Panditji, see, he wasn't aware," Anjana chuckled.

"Deepak, why don't you go take a shower and then come down? Dinner would be served in ten minutes," Panditji said.

"Well, gentlemen, I have thought a lot after our conversation in the jail about our children's choices, especially when it comes to their marriage. While I still believe in marriage within the caste and sub-caste and community, I know times are changing, and they are changing faster than oldies like us can think," Panditji blurted it out quickly, took a short break, gulped a glass of water kept for him at the side table next to him, and continued his address with a beaming face, "I know Rajendra ji and his family are very good people and they have a very good family background. He is a self-made man, and he has his roots here in Patna, which date back several generations. So, for the sake of our kids and their shared future, I would request Chitra ji and Rajendra ji to agree to the marriage proposal of our son Deepak." He paused briefly, looked intently at Rajendra, then at Chitra, then at professor and then at the Shayar, both of whom nodded at him, and then he said, "Rajendra ji, Chitra ji, we wish to seek your consent to marry our son, Deepak, to your daughter Guria." Panditji said and waited with bated breath for Rajendra to respond.

Anjana was also quiet, standing beside Panditji with folded hands. They were both looking expectantly at Rajendra ji and Chitra *ji*, eagerly awaiting their approval.

Rajendra looked towards Chitra, and then towards his other friends. They all nodded their approvals.

"Panditji, you have given us great honour in asking for the hand of our daughter for your son. I am slightly surprised though, as this is our first meeting with our families, and I had thought we would slowly get to know one another." He got up with folded hands, positively surprised, and went and hugged Panditji. He then said, "I have nothing to refuse, and I am floored by this gesture from Panditji and Anjana ji. It is the sweetest surprise I have had in years, and that I had no clue it would happen. I knew that Panditji had slightly different way of doing things, probably he has learnt his lessons well as a police officer, but I feel extremely happy and relieved for my daughter. Deepak is a good boy and Guria could not have gotten a better life partner. In Deepak, I have seen an effective manager and a hungry businessman who was also ethical to the core." Chitra got up and hugged Anjana thanking her profusely, after which both took Najma in an embrace. There was quite an uproar in the house and people were congratulating one another. Rajendra got emotional, and added, "Guria has been brought up with a lot of love and care, and Chitra has done a wonderful job in preparing her for life beyond our home. I hope and pray that she does everything possible to gel nicely in your household and contribute in her own little way to your happiness. We are proud parents, and we hope that she would make us proud in the future too."

Deepak came out quickly after his bath, having heard quite an uproar, half-suspecting the news Panditji himself gave him, in front of the entire troupe. He was speechless.

Life had come a full circle for him. He had been wishing to speak about this with his father for almost two years, but he could never find the resolve or the correct opportunity to do so. And yet, without him having to directly confront his parents, or even try to convince them, his dream had come true. He went around touching the feet of all the elders and taking their blessings. He also went to Kul gave him a big tight hug. Kul then called up Guria and broke the news to her. Guria could not utter a word. She was surprised to the core. She had just spent an entire evening in the park thinking aloud about her strategy in the event in case Deepak did not speak to his father. Kul handed over the phone to his brother.

Deepak took the phone and excused himself to go to the veranda and talk to his bride-to-be, until he was called back by Anjana for dinner.

The Professor was at his verbose best. He gave a two-minute speech on the changing society and the changing culture of India and was highly appreciative of Panditji's well thought out step. Panditji had kept the happiness and future of his son and daughter-in-law above all the concerns of caste and creed, despite his ingrained belief against such marriages. He had chosen love and happiness over all such cultural and social bindings. He became a father, that every father could be inspired by and proud of. The Shayar too gave his blessings to Deepak. It was an excellent dinner, both food and atmosphere wise, and afterwards all the guests went back happy and content.

The Professor was happy that he could witness the event and he promised to return for the engagement ceremony, which was to be held soon.

It had turned out to be the best night so far, in Deepak and Guria's lives.

Chapter 22
1975

"Nilima, look who is here!" Nilima's father-in-law, Dr. A. N. Sahay, called as Professor Dhiraj Sahay arrived at the house.

Nilima ran towards the lobby area, overjoyed to see her husband after such a long time. She touched his feet and took his briefcase. Then she hurriedly went into the kitchen and brought a cup of tea with milk and sugar. The Professor liked his tea that way and was elated to see his parents, his wife, his kids, and his larger joint family.

Theirs was and had always been a joint family. Dr. A. N. Sahay was an illustrious figure in Bihar and Jharkhand. He had retired as a long-serving Principal of the Patna Law College and was thereafter made the Registrar of the Magadha University, post which he had served for a long-time as the Principal of the newly incorporated Ranchi Law College. He was a powerful speaker and had a remarkable penchant for humour. Despite his old age, he was in good health and had kept himself in great shape. He always had a queue of people visiting him every day for some issue or the other, and it was his motto in life that no visitor should go back without food and tea. It was believed in general that one *chulha* in the house was to be kept warm throughout the day, just to prepare tea for everyone who would come to see Dr. Sahay.

The Professor freshened himself up and then narrated the stories about his time in prison, his new-found friends, and the fact that he was party to a proposed marriage of two youngsters.

It was a lovely time for the Sahay family. The entire family was together after a long time, and it all felt so complete. The men of the house were hugely interested in politics, and they loved to debate upon the subject, often shouting their lungs out to get their point across and win the political battle of the day.

Their house itself was like a democratic country where everyone, be it young or old, had a right to put forth their opinion. They were total non-vegetarians and loved having eggs and mutton liver for breakfast, chicken or mutton for lunch, and a bird for dinner. The ladies of the house had maids and cooks at their disposal, but they also liked to do things on their own.

Nilima and her elder sister-in-law, whom she used to address as *jiji*, were very good at cooking and managing the entire household. They were not only good cooks but were swift and efficient in their culinary skills and had the ability to give famous chefs a run for their money.

Dr. A. N. Sahay believed in a maxim, possibly created by himself: "*Nothing better than Muslim food, cooked in a Hindu kitchen, and served on a Christian dining table*". He loved his food and the time he spent with people of all ilks, his friends, family members, and acquaintances. He was also very fond of children and always spent a lot of time with them.

He had an incredibly sharp memory and he had learnt Shakespeare so well that he could, at any given time, narrate verses or dialogues from any page of a Shakespearean play at will. He could also tell the page number in which the dialogue could be found. He also remembered a Keats or a Shelly by heart and could quote them verbatim.

He had told the Professor not to worry about his job as something would spring up sooner than later. He was well connected with the powers at the university level and the Professor was a well-known teacher of his subject. Dr. Sahay wanted him to take up a role at Ranchi itself, rather than going back to Simdega, for he wished to spend more time with his son and his family.

Dr. Sahay's wife, the granny of the house, was not well for a few years then, and was bed-ridden. She was euphoric to see the Professor, who sat beside her for a while, had his tea slowly beside her. Her room was full of her children and grandchildren whom she kept blessing. The Professor was also glad to be back, and his kids did not leave him the entire day.

He was elated at the thought of having created true and, hopefully, an everlasting friendship with three other gentlemen, one of whom, the Shayar, he had known for a while!

Chapter 23
1975

"Hi Guria. What's up? You must have been tired yesterday after our engagement," Deepak enquired, over the phone.

"It was not tiring at all, Deepak. I absolutely loved it. Babu was a little sad that the Professor and his wife could not make it, but they have assured him that they will come for the wedding. Overall, it was excellent. I guess the personal rapport of our parents clinched the deal for us. You had not even brought it up to Panditji yet, right? Babu was in prison where Panditji was the jailor, so we thought it was all messed up. However, it turned out so nicely. Full marks to their new friends, the Shayar ji and Professor saheb," Guria said, wisely.

"Yes, it's amazing to see how things turn. It must be some good karma of my previous births that I'm getting married to you. I am so thankful to God for it."

"I totally agree with you, Deepak. It would have been very difficult to get a girl like me without good karma over multiple births. So, you must always remember that you have earned me, and you should treat me like a diva all your life. So, should we say, ours is a *karmic* connection?"

"You are mischievous. I am happy that you are not my boss anymore, because our big boss is back in business!"

"Absolutely! We need his magic wand. We were slipping in numbers, despite our best efforts. We must have been doing something wrong. Let Babu detect it and teach us. We are better prepared to learn his lessons now, having managed the business for a few months."

"So, what's the plan tonight? Can we meet up?"

"Let us give it a while. We have just been engaged and our families are watching us closely. I have not been able to spend time with Babu ever since he was released, for everything has been so sudden and hectic. Let's meet sometime later, maybe next week or so."

"I agree. It is difficult though. We really should get married as soon as possible, but who would tell that to our parents? They want to do it in December. It is a long wait, and I am not prepared for it. I cannot remain away from you for so long," Deepak said in a soft and romantic voice.

"Oh, I know, sweetheart. Let's see how it goes. *Chalo*, I'll see you tomorrow at office. Bye!"

Guria disconnected the phone and went to sit near her father.

"So, beta, I hope you are happy," Rajendra asked.

"Yes, Babu. I'm very happy, and you know that! Don't tease me now. Just tell me how it happened? How did you manage it for me?"

"I did not know it would turn out this way," Rajendra said. "It is all God's blessings. In fact, up until a couple of days before the end of our prison term, I was not even aware that Deepak is Panditji's son and neither did he know that you are my daughter. In the same conversation, one day, we got into a massive debate on caste and creed and whether love marriages should be allowed. Panditji was dead against marriages outside caste. However, I got huge support from the Professor and the Shayar. In fact, towards the end, the Shayar lamented rather passionately, that he did not have a child and was so unhappy because of it, while people who had children were not bothered about their long-term happiness and were busy trying to protect their archaic customs and beliefs.

"Well, it could have gone the other way. Panditji's position could have hardened. I sensed it and got up to go back to my barrack. The others also ended the discussion midway. Nobody's ego was hurt, and he got his time to think through and take a decision. I think my call to bring Professor saheb to our house also crystallised the decision and quickened the meeting to finalise the wedding. I guess Panditji wanted to be on the right side of the discussion and take a stand as a friend and as a father. He is an amazing man. He has realised that he is also a father and that it is his responsibility to keep his children happy. I hope and I pray that God bless you both, beta."

"All that happens is for the good. But it would have been so much better had Amit not gone through this pain.

I feel so bad for him, Babu," Guria said, with a tear in her eyes.

"We can never comprehend God's ways, Guria. Sometimes, it looks like we have been wronged and we ask ourselves: why us?" Rajendra was almost in tears. He was upset but he was a God loving person and he knew there was always something good in what happens. It could have been worse. He knew that Amit was a strong boy, and he would do well for himself in his life.

"We must accept it as a 'fait-accompli' and move ahead in our lives. We should try to give him comfort, happiness, and encouragement."

"What's cooking between father and daughter, huh? You guys cannot keep me away from all these discussions. Oh, you guys are literally crying! Lots of bonding happening here, I suppose!" Chitra said, coming into the room.

"No, Mumma. We were just talking about God's blessings, and the strange ways in which they get showered upon us. Come here, join us!" Guria got up to get Chitra to sit next to her dad. She sat on the opposite side, and she could see both her parents in a single frame. She loved having a chat with both and this was one of those days she could just sink in and let the world move forward. Before that, she had thought about asking her father about their business issues. He was also a bit relaxed, and he had some time on him. But she thought the better of it and postponed her office discussions for the next day.

"Babu, I'll tell you what we have been able to achieve at work in your absence tomorrow at office. Let us enjoy this evening together, for now. I'll call Amit too. You guys wait over here. Amit! Amit!" Guria chirped in her lovely voice.

"I am so happy for Guria. You have managed it beautifully. A problem got converted into an opportunity. You made him your friend in jail and were able to move things slowly, but decisively! Your game-plan worked," Chitra said.

"Yes, Chitra. It was a well thought out strategy. We had clarity in terms of knowing the details beforehand, and it worked effectively! Thanks for all your help." Now that was a masterstroke Guria's parents had played for their daughter and her life with Deepak. They knew it was a marriage made in heaven and they had to make it happen. There was no better way, in hindsight. Now there was a lot of work to be completed for the marriage to happen.

Chitra came to Guria's room and said, "Beta, there is some good news I wish to share. There was a conversation between the three friends that started during the engagement itself. While initially they were good to have the marriage ceremony in December, which was still a good six odd months away, it seems that Panditji got the dates checked and there is a date available after just a fortnight. The three friends made up their minds to get the marriage executed on the 27th of the month of June. They checked in with the Professor, and he gave his consent too. He would travel for the marriage with his spouse."

Guria had no words to express. She knew that they were the least prepared for the marriage. But she was overjoyed, and she bubbled with excitement. Chitra saw Guria and hugged her. They both got emotional. Guria ran to meet her dad. Rajendra hugged her and told her to get cracking. She had a lot of shopping to do.

Guria called up Deepak again. Deepak did not know about the new dates.

"Deepak, are you aware of the new dates?"

"What new dates? Have they pushed our marriage back to next year?" Deepak felt on the edge.

"I guess so. Mom told me it is getting pushed to next year summers," Guria winked, which Deepak could obviously not see.

He retorted, "How can they? Are they not our parents? What are they up to? Ummm, wait! I know you are pulling my leg. Yes, I can feel you laughing with your teeth out. Don't try to fool me," Deepak said in a slightly raised voice. Guria felt his heartbeat rising.

She excitedly told him about the new dates and that she was going to be very busy with her shopping as the time was way too limited.

Deepak felt ecstatic. He wanted to meet Guria that evening. Guria told him she would meet him only on the day of the marriage. She did not have time and she had a lot of work. Deepak understood. He however told her he could help her with her shopping. Guria told him she would seek his help if only she needed or desired it.

Deepak pestered with his request. He wanted to at least buy her the sari for her marriage. Guria felt good about it but told him she would do as advised by her parents, and he should exactly do as per his own parents wish. Both knew their parents had thought the best for their future and could take the best decisions for them. They knew the ceremonies and they knew what needed to be done. There was a lot of work going ahead.

Chapter 24
1975

"Hello! So now, we are officially in-laws. Don't forget, I represent the girl's side in this marriage, for I am staying with my wife at Rajendra ji's residence," the Professor said, giving a warm hug to Panditji.

"Yes, I know. The Shayar is here and will be from our side," Panditji said. "Najma ji has been helping Anjana for the last three days to sort out everything. She has worked like a horse. I feel indebted to all of you, for you guys have made our lives so much fun." Panditji said with a hint of his voice wavering. He continued emotionally, "Finally, in my life, I can say that I have three friends who are like my soulmates and who understand me thoroughly. I know that the three of you would be with me in happiness and in crisis." Panditji looked quizzically at all his friends, who looked back and then they hugged one other. Everyone went to take care of their assigned work.

After a while, Panditji and the Professor walked towards the garden area, and Panditji said, "With you around, I would be able to meet any challenge with open arms and overcome it confidently. Think of this as your own house and relax."

The Professor was overwhelmed with Panditji's loving words, and he responded in his signature style. He shook hands with Panditji, and said, "We are friends for life now, and I would do all it takes to keep us four together, through thick and thin in our lives."

Panditji beamed, took the Professor in a tight embrace, nodding at him, and took him inside the house. They saw the Shayar. The guests had arrived from either side. Deepak looked handsome and he was seated on the *Maharaja* chair meant only for the bride and the groom. He was flocked by his cousins and friends. They were chatting with him. He felt a bit lost as he kept waiting for Guria to appear. He wanted to see her come into the reception area in her bridal *lehenga*. He knew that she would be decked up. He did not wish to miss the once-in-a-lifetime opportunity. His wait was over within minutes, as Guria came into the reception area, with Amit, her parents, and the Professor and his wife at her side.

Deepak stood up from the chair, agape at the ethereal beauty of his soon-to-be bride. He felt deep gratitude and an overpowering love for his beloved. In that moment, cameras went click-a-click with powerful flashlights. There was one cameraman from the groom's side and the other from the bride's side.

If you would know, cameras in those days were not easy like the mobile cameras of today that can click continuous burst of shots, edit them, and delete as per requirement. They had reels that needed to be processed at a studio. Only photographers had those equipments. Those were technologically challenged times!

The reaction of the groom was captured with his jaws dropped at the first look of his bride. Guria saw Deepak and flushed. She had a smile on her face. Normally she would wink at Deepak, and she wished to, but she knew someone's camera would capture that. She thought better and looked askance, taking in the crowd of friends and relatives around her. She folded her hands and nodded at her elders in the function. Amit and Chitra raised her lehenga slightly so she could walk properly.

Deepak got teased by his sisters, as they were hysterical at his reaction to Guria's entry. Deepak felt agitated at himself. He knew he could have done better, but he felt good immediately as Guria came and sat beside him. She was wearing a light pink lehenga which had a lot of work all over. It was beautiful and must have been expensive. She wore jewellery that was not over the top, but understated with 18-carat diamonds studded in. She wore bangles in her hands, a tiny diamond stud on her nose, and a *kamardhani* studded with rubies and emeralds. It accentuated her womanly curves, and she looked stunning.

As the people settled and waited to go to the stage to shower the bride and the groom with their blessings and their gifts, the Professor spoke to the Shayar, "Farooqui saheb, should I announce a recital by you, just a small fifteen-minute session, as blessings for our children? We have some time before the *mandap* gets set up for the wedding."

"It will be my honour, Professor saheb. Please check with Rajendra Babu and Panditji first, as they might have some ceremonies now."

"I have already spoken to them!" Professor said and moved towards the microphone in the hall. He took the mic and said, 'It is my honour to invite on stage, the Shayar Umar Farooqui. I believe all of you have heard his shayari and nazms, at some point or the other in your lives. It is our good fortune that he is here as one of the closest friends of Panditji. Shayar ji, please grace the stage!"

"*Izzat bakshne ke liye shukriya!* Arz kiya hai…" said the Shayar.

"Irshaad, irshaad!" said the crowd.

"Ik gul sa naqsh-o-nigar tera,
Bholi si teri soorat,
Rooh teri ruhani si,
Jao tum mujhe aise na benaqaab karo,
Jao tum mujhse aise na gila karo;
Jao tum mujhse aise na shikva karo,
Machalte hain teri madhoshi pe,
Machlate hain teri kamsin jawaani pe,
Machalte hain tere lab ko chhoo ke,
Machalte hain teri kasak se;
Machalte hue hum gharq hone lagte hain;

Machalta chhod hamein tum aise na rusva karo;
Tere dar par hum tere ishq mein fanaa ho jayenge,
Tere dar par aaj hum jannat ko choom aayenge;
Teri nazar se gire ek ashq ko chura loon, saki,
Aaj phir tera deedar kar khud ko bacha loon saki;
Yeh fariyaad tum sun lo meri,
Tere rukhsar ki lali mein hum aaj fanaa ho jayenge."

(Your face is like a flower,
You have an innocent look;
Your soul is spiritual,
Do not unmask me like this;
Do not complain to me like this,
Do not have such grouse against me;
I quiver when I see you intoxicated,
I quiver when I see your youth;
I quiver as I touch your lips,
I quiver at your pain;
Heart wrenchingly I drown,
Don't leave me dishonoured while I writhe;
I would be destroyed in your love, at your doorstep,
I would kiss paradise at your doorstep;
Let me steal one drop of tear from your eyes,
Let me save myself again by seeing your face;
Please hear this entreaty of mine,
Let me get destroyed by the redness of your cheeks.)

"Wonderful! Wonderful! Shayar Farooqui, let's hear one more nazm."

"People, I am done here! Professor saheb, the stage is all yours. Greetings. Good night!"

"Thank you, Shayar Farooqui! Your nazm has touched all of our hearts. Thanks for entertaining everyone with this soulful rendition," the Professor said, and looked towards the guests and folded his hands, saying, "I would request all of you to have the food. It has been prepared with a lot of love and effort. Please bless the lovely couple, Guria and Deepak! Thank you!" The professor kept the microphone and went to bless the couple. Nilima went along with the Professor. They were one of the first couple to bless the couple. Both Deepak and Guria got up, touched their feet and showed their deepest gratitude. They were blessed and showered with the choicest gifts. There was a queue to bless the couple, and it took some guests up to an hour to bless. A lot of people went towards the dinner counter, and they were served with delicious north indian delicacies. The food was vegetarian, but exquisite. The evening had just started.

Guria and Deepak were taken from the reception area after the blessings ceremony for a quick dinner. They were surrounded by their friends, and colleagues. While Deepak had a hearty meal with his friends, Guria took a few bites. She could not eat much but she felt good. She knew the rituals would begin soon, and they would possibly continue right through the night, into the dawn.

Chitra, Anjana, and Nilima took care of the rituals. Najma kept the crowd entertained, having goaded the two sides to play *Antakshari*.

The wedding rituals took over four hours and it was finally time for Guria to go to her in-law's place. It was a heartrending moment for everyone, including the groom's family. Guria cried like a four-year-old and she had to be literally taken away by her brother to her husband's swanky new car. She sat beside Deepak, and the car left for Deepak's house. They were followed by multiple cars, in which Panditji, Anjana, and the others went.

The Shayar and the Professor stayed back for a bit at Rajendra's residence. They consoled Chitra and Rajendra. It was a tradition that had gone on for centuries in India, and it withstood the test of time. Rajendra's house looked deserted, while Panditji's house looked all set to welcome the newly married couple.

Panditji decided to call all his friends for a reception the next evening and sent special invitation to his friends. It was an evening to remember for Rajendra and Chitra as they were the guests of honour. It was a lovely evening, and Guria's parents were always sitting close to their daughter. Guria laughed and cried that evening, hysterically at times, as her new life kicked in. She had ceremoniously moved to her husband's house, having left the house of her parents. It was a new world, but she wished to keep her husband's house intact, and she took it upon herself to keep the family happy.

Chapter 25

1975

Two days after the wedding, the four families travelled to Bodh Gaya and were put up in a guest house organised by Panditji. Guria and Deepak had gone to Goa to celebrate their honeymoon, and their parents planned this friendly trip for the families to Bodh Gaya, a religious place near Patna.

Bodh Gaya was the place where Gautam Buddha had achieved Enlightenment, and it was famous amongst Buddhists from all over the world. It had always been a religious site for Indians. A lot of Hindus consider Buddhism and Jainism as offshoots of Hinduism. These faiths took their pupils away from ritualism, that Hinduism eventually started to practice. India being a secular country, allowed for people of all faiths to coexist and visit these places of high religious importance.

The year that saw the birth of a tyrannical rule in the country, brought forth some good times as well for the four families, and this trip served as a welcome break for all the four couples.

They checked into the guest house around one in the afternoon and had a pre-arranged lunch. Then, they decided to have a quick nap in their rooms. They had planned to go out for site visits around four in the afternoon and had hired a small bus so that all of them could travel together.

"Panditji, let's first go to the Mahabodhi Temple. It is a must-see place," Rajendra said, in a manner that implied a certain authority on religious matters.

"I agree with you, Rajendra ji. See, I am not calling you *Samdhi ji,* as we are friends first and samdhis later," Panditji chuckled.

"You guys better solemnise being in-laws," the Shayar remarked.

"Ha ha ha! Let's go to the Mahabodhi Temple. From there, we can see if we have enough time for any other site visits tonight. Else, we can have dinner at a nice restaurant and get back for an evening full of fun with cards and shayari and songs," the Professor suggested.

"Farooqui is on leave, request for poetry will not be entertained," the Shayar quipped.

"We will not trouble you, *Miya* Farooqui!" Rajendra said, with a smile.

"Let's get down here. We would have to walk a few steps to be inside the temple complex. We will get back here if someone is somehow running late," Rajendra said and looked at others. Everyone nodded their agreement, and they slowly started walking towards the temple complex. "Let us walk together and pray together. May Lord Buddha, the Enlightened One, show us the right path and guide us in future! May Lord Buddha take us all to the path of *Nirvana*!" said Panditji.

They went inside the temple complex and came out after two hours. The temple was built around the original Bodhi tree, under which Lord Buddha had meditated and attained Nirvana. The original Bodhi tree was not there anymore, but its descendants were very much there, and the tallest tree was now eighty feet in height.

Next, they went to see the giant Buddha statue, just a kilometre away. The statue looked beautiful and serene. It was made of intricately carved sandstone and red granite. The walk was tiresome, but the buzzing activity in the vicinity of the temple kept them going. After the prayers were over, ladies wished to go to the nearby Tibetan refugee market. They were dropped off at the market and the men went ahead towards their guest house. They would wait for their wives to get back and then go out for dinner together.

The four ladies thoroughly enjoyed their time shopping and bought a generous number of winter-wear, souvenirs, and handicrafts. Later in the night, they had their dinner at a nearby four-star hotel before returning to their guest house.

Panditji footed the dinner bill, saying that Rajendra ji had managed most of the functions, not allowing him to spend for the marriage at all. So, this was his chance for repayment. In fact, he said that the entire trip would be sponsored by him, and no one had to spend on either food or travel.

The Professor and the Shayar appreciated his gesture while Rajendra kept trying to pay, wherever possible.

The next day they went to the Thai Monastery, the Royal Bhutan Monastery, Muchalinda Lake, Chinese Temple, and Jama Masjid.

Back at the guest house, the Shayar told the group that he was fed up with the ongoing political scenario in India.

He said, "I would work towards educating my fellow religious thought leaders and the general Muslim populace to desist from voting for the current dispensation in the next elections, whenever it was held. The government could not afford to continue imposing an Emergency for perpetuity. The government has to reverse the Emergency at some time in the future and elections are a given. I cannot emphasise enough that for whatever reason, Muslims have voted in sync for the parties or candidates of their choice. Congress has mostly been on the receiving end of all these votes, although in some states at certain points in time, voting could have gone differently. This is an important reason for the appeasement policy instituted by most of the political parties.

"I want to work with the common people to emphasise the need to remove the government of the day, in the next elections. I do not see many improvements happening in India for the common people. A lot of things could be done for the overall improvement of a nation during an autocratic rule. However, with the Emergency in place, I, for one, cannot see much happening. In my mind, the 20-point program of the government or the 5-point program of the ruler would not achieve much."

The others nodded in agreement. They knew that the Shayar was in a different kind of flow and they did not wish to break his chain of thoughts. The conversation was close to the hearts for all the men in the room.

"As soon as I get back, I want to get into a political career—not for its gains, but to help my community avoid its pitfalls. I might have to travel frequently for that and may not always be available for our lovely morning tea-sessions, but you must know that I am always there for all of you," the Shayar declared, rather emotionally.

"This is wonderful! Just keep yourself safe. I agree with you wholeheartedly. This is the best you can do to give back to your community," The Professor said with a lot of conviction.

Then Rajendra said, "Education is the key here. We are with you in this fight and whenever required, you can count on us. We would stand united, to support you and our nation," Panditji assured.

It was a lovely trip for the four couples, and they had a *rangarang karyakram* with songs and sher-o-shayari during their return trip to Patna. Nilima sang a few soulful songs from her favourite Lata Mangeshkar collection along with a couple of *bhajans*. Her rendition was so good that Panditji touched her feet saying that *Saraswati Maa* was perched on her *jihva*. Nilima was embarrassed at the gesture, but everyone went with the flow. They had no doubt in what Panditji had said, and everyone agreed that they were privy to the best rendition of the bhajans. Panditji explained to the group, "A lot of people can sing well. However, not everyone can be a bhajan singer. There are many bhajan singers who don't have any *rasa* or *bhava*. I am surprised to see that *bhabhi ji* has both rasa and bhava and her voice is like God's own voice. Bhabhi ji, you should sing a lot more and you should go for the *bhajan sandhya* in our state. You would soon become a national treasure."

"If only Professor saheb wanted that!" Nilima said, a tad ruefully, before quickly adding, "I am, however, very happy with my present role as a homemaker and a mother. I have a lot to do, and I do not have any ambitions for myself."

Chapter 26
1976

The Shayar was in the vicinity of Delhi's Jama Masjid. He was engaged in meetings over the last few days with various Muslim thought leaders. He had also attended many sessions in the bungalows of his political associates. They were all worried about the news from the infamous Dujana House. It had become popular for conducting many botched operations, wherein people had died without a trace. They just disappeared. To make matters worse, the vasectomy operation was being carried out by force, by the government authorities.

The Dujana House was a big headache, as lots of young and old people alike, from largely the minority community, were being targeted for tubal ligation, vasectomy, and sterilization. They were being offered three hundred rupees in exchange for undergoing the operation. A lot of poor Muslims agreed to do so in the dire need for money.

The Shayar was against the compulsory relocation of a large section of the minority from their shanties in the Turkman Gate area. This was being done to clear the mess of the slum, to give the area the cleanliness that a large city required. The municipal authorities had given Demolition notices to many households in the area, saying that they needed to move to a location at the outskirts of the city. The Shayar, along with other thought leaders met the Municipal Commissioner against this demolition drive and requested him to allow the people of Turkman Gate to move to a nearby slum. The Commissioner, however, rejected their appeal and went on with the demolition notices.

The Shayar felt deeply troubled by this, so with his troupe of almost a hundred volunteers, he was at the forefront of a fight against these governmental policies. He took his battle to the streets and went on a door-to-door campaign to educate the people against tubectomy and vasectomy. He also counselled them against their movement from their homes to the outskirts of Delhi. He tried to make them understand the fact that their lives will become difficult in the outskirts, as they would have to travel to Delhi every day to find work, thereby spending a lot of money on transport. They were poor people, and the Shayar knew that they would not survive if they spent most of their meagre earnings on transport itself.

"Shayar Farooqui, thank you for coming to meet us. Please help us fight all this injustice the government has brought down upon us. Are you aware that the Dara Mia did not even come back after that operation at Dujana House?"

The Shayar sat with a thud in a rickety chair inside the 5*5 tin-shed, that the poor called their home. He comforted the woman who might have been in her late thirties, but looked almost sixty, because of the ordeals of living a life not meant for people. The life of a person who was below the poverty line, could be anything but decent, and they had to do more than others for merely surviving the day. Two square meals were not possible, so they kept loins of cloth tied to their stomach, moistened with water, so that the hunger would not stop them in their tracks. They lived a life shorter than the normal, and some gave up earlier than the others.

Shayar looked at the lady with moist eyes and told her that he knew about Dara Mia. He knew that the authorities in Dujana House denied that he had even visited the place or had gone there for any operation. The other men who had gone with him returned, but Dara Mia was nowhere to be found. "What should we do to protect our men? We don't need their three hundred rupees. We are happy on our own. Please save our houses from demolition, Shayar Farooqui. Please help us organise ourselves," the woman cried out to him.

The Shayar heard the same tale like a broken vinyl record from multiple people. He felt dejected and greatly pained at their troubles. He told them to show fierce opposition to the authorities when they came for the demolitions. He also told them that he would take the fight to the authorities at Dujana House, and would not allow them to continue this racket of sterilization. They had no authority to play with the right to procreate, given by God to human beings. It was blasphemy and the government must surrender.

The municipal authorities were supposed to get there the following day for carrying out the demolition drive. But the Shayar did not believe that the government would go through with it without another round of notices and meetings, especially when none of the residents had moved yet. It had been a long yet successful day. The Shayar and his team of strategists had created a plan to foil the demolition drive. He was part of a larger group of people from his community. He was being helped by the *maulvis* and the politicians from across the spectrum, albeit the help was with a precondition of silence. The Shayar knew he had to wage the battle against the brutality of the authorities and report it to the police. He was prepared for a pitched battle of nerves with the government. He felt that their resistance, although without arms, was enough to make the government backtrack. Even during the Emergency, the government could not be seen being unfair and partial to the rich, and completely against the poor.

He spoke to his wife, Najma, in the evening. He told her not to be worried as he had fortified himself and his team of protestors, against any punitive action by the government forces. Najma counselled him and told him not to be in the forefront of the fight against the powers. She told him that they were too powerful and as a citizen, they had no rights left in the country. The government could do as per its own will, as it was already visible across the country. The Shayar told her not to worry and to seek help from his friends, if required. He also told her he would be back within a few days.

Najma spoke to Rajendra and Panditji. They were also worried. They spoke to the Professor. It was a tough night for all of them. They could not sleep. They could not do a lot in any case. Not much news filtered those days in India. The freedom of the press was compromised and especially such news got suppressed for longer than the usual time. News filtered slowly through the activities of some of the opposition party leaders, but it was few and far between. Radio had become the mouthpiece of the government, and it broadcasted stuff that was pre-approved by the Information & Broadcasting Ministry. The I&B Ministry was one of the most powerful ministries in those days.

The Shayar thought to himself, unable to sleep, about what all could happen the very next day at Turkman Gate. He would be there as a warrior, protecting his tribe from the atrocities of the government, should such a need arise. He would be there more as a counsel against any misstep by the authorities.

He had an ill feeling in his mind, the next day would be no different, or would it be?

Chapter 27
1976

The Shayar was at the forefront of the fight against the demolition of the shanties of Turkman gate. The locals had organised a resistance against the demolitions by creating a three-fold resistance matrix. In the second ring of defence, there was a group of youths who would throw brickbats at the police and the municipal authorities, and would not allow the bulldozers to move forward by hurling stones and other objects at them.

If, however, the plan failed, and they were able to move forward nullifying the second line of defence, there was a third ring of resistance. This would be fierce. Women and children would be lying down on the road to stop the bulldozers from moving forward. Elderly women would be at the front, followed by younger women and children.

The political leadership representing the slums, which included thought leaders and learned people like the

Shayar, were a part of the team that had created this resistance. This leadership was supposed to be standing at the very front of Turkman Gate, as the first line of defence, to reason with the police and the municipal authorities and ask for a second round of meetings and fresh dates.

The wait was unending, and it felt like a century had gone by since the morning. But there was still no sight of those dreaded bulldozers. Some of the youngsters were happy that the police might have missed the action date, or they might have orders to move the dates forward. The Shayar was circumspect, having seen the iron hand of the police in the near past, in Patna and elsewhere. There was some optimism growing within the crowd and many more people came to the eviction site, showing their support for the human rights. A group of senior leaders, however, did not accept the theory. They felt it was only a ploy by the police to initiate fatigue in the ranks of the street soldiers. Also, it would take the police only a couple of hours to decimate the area of its unworthy, shabby, and poor homes that gave dreams of the downtrodden, wings of gold. The poor and the downtrodden in India were as much a part of the independence movement as anyone else. They were made to believe by the leaders that there was only one solution to their plight, and that was the independence of the country from the British empire. It had been many a decade since independence, but the poor remained poor, while the rich gained riches beyond measure.

The country had seen wealth in the hands of a few ultra-rich, a rising middle class, which was mostly in the services, but also an ever bulging, below poverty line group of people. They were hand-to-mouth and had to dig for their food every day, else they would die in the graves made of their own digging. This move at Turkman Gate showed a downright disregard to the cause of the poor by the forces. Rehabilitation was not planned properly, but the orders of eviction were plastered on the walls of the ill-fated colony.

To think of the plight of the common man in a situation like this makes one shudder in disbelief. Imagine what happened that day, will you? Well, let me make it easy for you and narrate it further here. Check for the authenticity of this piece yourself, though. A literary license to modify the events has been taken by the author here.

Suddenly, a boy came running in and alerted everyone that the policemen were marching towards Turkman Gate along with four bulldozers. There was also a large contingent of officials along with the police. Suddenly there was heightened activity. This was the time when reasoning could work. The police could take a step back on seeing the three lines of defence and it would be impossible for them to move the bulldozers forward. After all, it was their own countrymen whose lives were on the line here, literally and figuratively.

The authorities approached Turkman Gate and were *gheraoed* by the thought leaders and the political leaders. In response, the cops showed an uncharacteristic resolve in following their orders. They immediately rounded up the so-called thought leaders, put them into a police van, and sent them to a nearby police station. The Shayar was one of the leaders who was rounded up and removed from the site of resistance, and he knew that there was something badly amiss. The heart of the nation had sunk to its lowest ebb, and it would be difficult to get it back. He felt a deep angst in his heart, an unrelenting pain, and he felt enraged at the situation of his mother land. He had truly lost his voice that day, in a nation of millions. For the teeming millions were under an autocratic rule, inconceivably so, from what people believed should happen in a democracy. The nation was on a warpath against her own citizens, the citizens who had dreamt of a powerful nation, free from its ills and poverty, marching ahead in all its glory.

While the Shayar could not find his voice that day, and could not narrate all he thought, he composed a heart-rending nazm in the prison they were held in, on a piece of torn paper, soiled by the shoes of the thought leaders and politicians. It was a carefree paper. A paper free from the clutches of the autocracy, and happily it flew in the wind, that took it to the Shayar's hand. The paper had found its meaning that day, as much as the Shayar had found the meaning of autocracy that hour.

The paper was scribbled on using a borrowed pen,

"Hindustan ka kya haseen khwab dikhaya tha
tumne ae Khuda,
Hum ko tumne khalibali kar rakha tha beete baras;
Mere khwab ki tabir mein tumne Hindustan ko ziba
aur maahru dikhaya tha,

Magar tumne kya naseeb bakhsha hai?
Yeh kaisa din tumne aaj dikhaya hai?
Ae Khuda aaj tum insaaniyat ko mat rusva karna,
Ae Khuda aaj tum insaan ko haivaaniyat se bacha lena;
Hum khuda ke bande tumse guzaarish karte hain,
Aaj tum insaniyat ko na rusva karna!"

(You showed us such a beautiful dream of India, Oh Lord,
You had transformed us into a carefree people in the bygone era;
An interpretation of my dreams told us that India was beautiful and splendidly luminous,
But what is it that is our destiny?
What kind of a day is it that you have shown us today?
Oh God, please do not disgrace humanity,
Oh God, please save mankind from inhuman thoughts;
We request you as your children,
Do not disgrace humanity today!)

The leaders of the movement against the demolition drive were kept in a prison cell overnight and were released the next morning. They were not given any information about any news from the Turkman Gate. After being released, the leaders went towards the site of action with no further delay. The Shayar was part of the congregation, and at that point they had only one wish. To see it all hunky-dory in the area. A wish that made their hearts bleed. A wish that made their hearts sink. They feared seeing a total destruction at the site. They feared for their friends and for the poor families, the kids and the women. They hoped against hope that all would be good, and all would be fine. The Shayar, for once, had turned positive. He brought only positive thoughts in his mind and castigated people if they spoke of any mass-scale tragedy.

The Shayar wanted to write about the resilience of his nation, of her people, and of the love they had for one another. He could not fathom how their own government could take such draconian decisions that would have a lasting impact on the lives of a multitude of the poor in the country. He knew in his heart, deep within, the country would come around, and that autocracy would slowly give way to a benign democracy. That would have been the best news possible.

But was it possible at all?

Chapter 28
1976

"Shayar Farooqui, I know that whatever has happened or at least whatever we have heard of, is just horrible. But do not be so quiet. Please tell us what you saw once you got back," Rajendra enquired, in a gentle and comforting tone.

"Dard-e-dil ke halaat kya bayaan karun?
Kaash woh subah kabhi na aayi hoti!"

(How do I express my heart's grief?
I wish that morning had never come!)

"*Janab*, tell us, please. We still don't know the details of what transpired in those forty-eight hours. As it is, we do not have any freedom for the press in our country," Panditji remarked.

"I sometimes feel ashamed to be an Indian," the Shayar said, in a grave voice. Rajendra and Panditji looked at each other as he spoke those words, not because of the gravity and pain they held but because his speech was devoid of the usual flair that his nazms and couplets had. He just spoke in a plain tongue, which was very unlike him.

"It feels like we are back to the days of colonial rule and are being subjugated in every way. In the name of beautifying our cities, we have taken steps that were clearly uncalled for. The Turkman Gate episode is the closest we have come to the Jallianwala Bagh massacre. Many people were left dead and maimed for life. The bulldozers just went forward, indiscriminately running over women and children. Hordes of people were arrested and sent for forced sterilisation, and several people appear to have never come back from the sterilisation camp in the nearby Dujana House. They possibly underwent botched operations and died on the spot, and were later cremated without their kin being informed about their death. I cannot even begin to explain how sad and horrified I feel today. In fact, I do not have any words and that's why I am not speaking in *Urdu*. I do not feel like speaking at all."

"Shayar Farooqui, I think we share your sadness. This is not the idea of India that we have or that we ever dreamt of. An India that would do to her citizens the same atrocities that the Queens' Army did is impossible to relate to," Panditji said in a deep, grave voice echoing the Shayar's thoughts. He got up slowly, took a few steps, came around towards his other two friends, and sat.

Rajendra also felt the Shayar's pain, and said, "I am also at a loss for words today. I understand that the topmost officials of the government were involved in this. The press did not carry the story even though it was widely seen by people who were present on the spot."

Panditji added his own assessment, saying, "This is the level of censorship we have in this country today. I have heard that the BBC knows a bit about this operation."

"I agree with both of you. This is not the India we ever wanted. Under the veil of the Emergency, these horrific crimes are being committed. Many of them might even go unchallenged in the Indian courts." Rajendra mulled over while speaking, and continued, "They would keep all the information to themselves and close it as a chapter, in their war against growing population and on cleaning up the cities. We must unite against this draconian law of the Emergency, and help JP lift the campaign again from scratch."

"Well, for one, I just hope and pray that the government announces elections sooner than later. And this time around, I sincerely hope that the poor of this country vote for a change," the Shayar said.

The three friends continued their talk about the ills of our democracy, of our nation, and of our models of governance. They also debated the benefits of a two-party democracy, and as to why our country ignored it and went for a multi-party democracy. They debated about the botched vision of our leadership, and the fact that the country needed a renaissance not only culturally, not only in an artistic fashion, but also morally and ethically. They knew there would be a backlash to the whip the government exercised in the name of the Emergency. They knew there would be a deeper resistance by the weak and by the poor. They knew the police baton had its limitations in a government for the people, by the people, and of the people.

"Miya Farooqui, you are a great person," Rajendra said. He continued, "Till now we used to think that you do not know how to speak our language, but I must say, you are very good at it. You are a learned man and a good human being. You feel the pain of other people and that is a great quality to have." He shifted comically in his chair and blew out his nose over his kerchief.

That was a comic relief for everyone, and Panditji said, "I have not seen Rajendra Babu shift in his chair in this fashion and blow his nose in public, earlier, ever." Rajendra looked at Panditji and then at the Shayar, and blurted out a big laugh, shaking and getting both his friends to join in.

India had lost her way and her people had lost their laughter in their near-normal lives. The friends were together that day for the next few hours, talking about their lives and about governance in that era. They committed to being foot soldiers in this war against tyranny. They agreed that they were no guinea pigs and they expected more from their nation. They agreed to lifting themselves once again and sounding the bugle against the autocratic rule. They shared a common vision for a great nation, and they were willing to fill the jails in the country, like many fellow Indians already were, to fight against the injustice being meted out to their countrymen.

There was a deep sense of hurt and anger.

"Yes, that's what. They cannot keep an entire country imprisoned! They would have to allow debate and discussions. They would have to allow a democratically elected government to come into power once again. This time around, please vote for even an unknown person, if they were to stand against the present dispensation," the Shayar said, and then added, "I feel guilty... I feel so guilty..."

"Why do you feel guilty, Shayar Farooqui? What could you have done from inside the prison? This sterilisation campaign will come here too. You must save your brothers. We all need to save ourselves and our people. Let's strategize. Let's call for support. Let's show them what we are capable of as a nation!" Panditji thundered.

"Panditji, you cannot participate in rallies as you are a government servant. Please calm down," Rajendra said.

"I would resign if it came to that. I would do all it takes but we need to throw away this autocratic way of governance, once and for all!" Panditji cried.

"Okay, alright, here. Let's not get too emotional and lose sight of the objective. We have our responsibilities both towards our families and our nation. But if we feel that our responsibility to our nation is at present more important than that which we have for our families, then we should go ahead. However, let us think it through."

" Shayar Farooqui, I know you are way too involved in this already. But please keep yourself at a safe distance for now. This government has a way to track and identify troublemakers and those so-called troublemakers could be thrown in an unseen hell-hole. Be careful. I am elder to all of you, and it is my strict advice," Panditji concluded, and they ended the meeting.

Chapter 29
1976

The room was full of the Agricultural Association members that day. It was seldom the case at any such opportunity in the recent past. The members were tense as they were on the receiving end of the governmental brickbats. They did not know whom to approach. Their usual support system in the bureaucracy had gone silent as they were under a strict vigil by the respective governments at the state level. They were under constant threats from the food inspectors and their team. The government had gone into business in a manner that was possibly not sustainable. The government took over the control of agricultural goods pricing, so that the farmer gets his due and the produce gets sold at the right price. The stockists were allowed to stock only as per the government approval, and not beyond. There were continuous raids by inspectors to verify the goods in the godowns. The traders were getting the stick from either end, as they had to take the produce at the prices set by the government, but they could not hoard beyond allowed quantities. Hoarding had become a bad word and it was increasingly difficult for the traders to make profits in their trade. They would survive, but they would not flourish if it continued for a few years.

"Who can help with our situation today? Can we make a representation and meet the authorities in the Agriculture Department or the Chief Minister?" one of the members of the committee asked, venting out his frustration.

"This way, we will collapse, and the present structure will crumble. We cannot continue for long in this manner," someone else mentioned in a demotivated tone.

"I have a different thought here. We cannot do much in the present situation," someone from the crowd said, and walked up towards the front to address the crowd. He was short heighted, bulky around the belly, and he seemed to be in the late sixties. He continued, "In fact, I believe, this is an honest period in our business. We have no power to hoard or to control the supply of the staples or of any other essential commodity. Therefore, what we can do is pass on the incoming cost with a nominal profit to the end-user. What it does is, it allows the government to control inflation through this mechanism."

While the conversation progressed, there was a young man, who looked radiant, and he probably had certain other thoughts. He was Deepak, the son-in-law of Rajendra ji. He stood up and spoke in an eloquent manner.

Deepak felt high inflation was not good for any country, and the governments' move was overall good for the economy, which had been in the doldrums for the better part of the last decade. The country was slowly but certainly converting into a socialist economy, and one did not quite understand how to charge a premium in the conventional trading business. He said, "So, if you wish to create fat profits, you must get into trading of non-essential commodities, or you must create some form of a set up where you could provide a different product. Essentially, what I'm saying is, create your factories to improve or change the product for the consumer." He paused for effect, allowed others to follow him, and continued, "For example, do not sell sugar alone; if possible, sell coated sugar candies. Do not sell rice but sell organic non-treated brown rice. Change the product composition and charge a hefty premium. That is the only business you could survive with, and generate a decent earning."

"What is your name, son? Give me your address or phone number," one of the older traders said.

"Well, I am sorry if I said something that I should not have said. My name is Deepak, and I am here to represent Rajendra ji and his trading firm." Deepak gave him his business card which also had his residence land-line number.

"No, not at all. Youth means a breath of fresh air. See, in front of so many of us who think we know our business better than others, you have given an out of the box solution," someone from the crowd complemented Deepak.

"We either think about your solution or quit thinking about decent profits altogether. We need to somehow sustain ourselves till elections are declared. We would be able to make a killing thereafter. Anyway, is Rajendra ji putting up a factory or what?" one of the committee members asked.

"As of now, sir, I don't think he is thinking of any such thing. These were my personal thoughts. I have read a lot about some of the articles that could be produced at a low initial set up cost, and I am thinking of putting up a factory that would process some of the agricultural goods, brand it, and sell it through distribution tie-ups," Deepak said.

"Okay, Deepak, could you help us understand your thought process better?"

"Yes sir. The question is, why can't we buy a good variety of top-grade wheat, process it to create *dalia* and *atta*, do a chic branding and packaging, and then sell it? I have studied its cost implications and profitability. We are talking about a business opportunity of continuous and sustainable growth in the cities. People do not have enough time to take their wheat to a store and get it converted to atta. Um…and the wheat converting guy always has tricks up his sleeves, so whichever quality of wheat you provide, your product looks almost the same and tastes bad. What I am proposing is a proper factory where we can control quality with a hawk-eye, create two to three varieties of atta, brand it and sell it as premium, a normal, and a variety for the poor. I think it will work. My calculations show that we could create a thirty per cent profit plus ROI business."

"What you're suggesting sounds like having a lot of potential. Can you help us set it up? Have you studied the capital cost for this factory? What if we are not able to convince people to buy this product and they continue with their old practices?"

"Well, sir, every business has its risks. Like in this factory, we would have Factory Inspectors and a host of such people. We would have to manage the external environment. My answer to you is that I have done my research, and I'm convinced about the product and the kind of factory I want to setup. The question is whether any one amongst you are convinced or not. But I guess, you need to do your own studies to be fully confident."

"Are you an employee at Rajendra ji's shop?"

"Yes, and a family member. I am his son-in-law," Deepak smiled.

There was suddenly a lot of arguments, counterarguments, and opinions put forth. Someone said that the police have decided to go around the slums of Patna and get people sterilised. Someone else suggested that there was no use setting up factories at this juncture, and people should instead concentrate on saving themselves and their kith and kin.

The government had taken an aggressive posture, and the freedom of citizens was at the receiving end. Population control was being taken way too seriously.

People were disturbed because their rights to progeny and to life were being taken away. For whatever it meant, a lot of Muslim associations and thought leaders had united under the same umbrella. Disparate groups were also coming together to fight the government tooth-and-nail, politically.

The population control measure that was being taken was somehow affecting people in the slums more than those who lived in urban houses. It also affected Muslims and *Harijans* more than others, and it was clear that these groups had been targeted. A section of intellectuals, which included professors and doctors among others, had already termed these steps as the most serious intervention ever, in the fight for population control.

However, they were not happy at the implementation methodology adapted by the government. According to them, the government had botched up its population control drive in more ways than one. The country could not remain a monarchy or an autocratic country forever and this population control program would go down as the worst implemented program, having done more harm than good, in the long-term.

A slow but silent unity of all the opposition parties was also in its formative years. The Janata Party, with obvious right wing and left-wing forces, was taking shape. The group was disparate and with completely different visions and agendas. However, in the face of the ongoing Emergency, they started working together.

Chapter 30

1976

Deepak was loitering in his home, feeling a bit dull that day. He had taken an off, while Guria had gone to work. Deepak wished to have some alone time, so he could decide what he wished to achieve from his life. He sat in the living area, in a relaxed pose, with his feet tucked under himself. He was softly singing along a tune he loved. It was playing on the radio in Lata Mangeshkar's melodious voice. He knew Lata's voice could never be replaced by anyone, never has been and never will be. He liked music from the early 1950s to the late 1970s. That was the time when the three biggies ruled Bollywood music—Mohd. Rafi, Kishore Kumar, and Mukesh. Lata had sung duets with all of them. Deepak also loved to hear *ghazals* by the three greats—Jagjit Singh, Ghulam Ali, and Mehdi Hassan. Mehdi Hassan normally sung in pure Urdu and Farsi languages. It was slightly difficult for the Indians to follow at times. However, Ghulam Ali, and more so, Jagjit Singh made the ghazals easy for Indians to understand and relate to. People had taken to shayari and nazms like never before and Deepak had acquired a decent taste in the same.

Suddenly, there was a shrill ring of the landline.

"Hello, is this Deepak?"

"Yes, I am Deepak. Who is it?"

"Hello Deepak, remember we met the other day at the Agriculture Association meeting?"

"Yes sir, I do remember having answered a couple of your questions. I hope all is good at your end. Let me know how I can help you."

"My name is Tarachand Kajaria. I have my own trading firm and have been in this business for generations now. We are doing decently, but the current situation has forced us to rethink. Would you mind meeting me? I could come to your house and pick you up in about fifteen minutes."

"Yes sir, not a problem at all. You could have just called me to your place, and I would have met you there itself. If you don't mind, why don't you come inside my house?"

"Well, I don't want to disturb your family. I also know that your father is a policeman, and I am always afraid of policemen," Tarachand chuckled.

"Do not worry about that. My father is not at home, and even if he were, there wouldn't have been a problem, I assure you of that. I insist, sir. Please do come in."

‘Okay, beta. I’ll be there in some time,” Tarachand said and disconnected the phone.

Deepak ran towards the main door and called out to his mother to prepare some snacks and tea.

After about twenty minutes, Tarachand helped himself inside the complex gate.

“You are welcome, sir! Please come in. We have a small house, but it is a very good home for us.”

“That is the most important thing in life, Deepak. The size of the house does not matter. What matters is the inhabitants of the house and whether they love and respect one another or not,” Tarachand said, as he stepped in.

“I see you have a lovely house with beautiful interiors. It seems like your mother has a very good taste. See, at the end of the day, it is the ladies of the house who make it a home.”

‘You are correct, sir. It is indeed the women who make a house a home. Please have a seat. Look, Mumma is here,” Deepak said and got up to take the tray from his mother.

Tarachand greeted Anjana with a namaste and after serving the tea and snacks, she went inside the kitchen, leaving Deepak and Tarachand to talk amongst themselves.

“Deepak, I wish to have a chat with you about your ideas and your future. I know you are already gainfully employed, but I have an offer for you. If you permit me, can I speak my mind?”

“Sure sir. I think you wanted to speak about my idea of setting up a factory to create value-accretive products from the staples and other essential agro-commodities.”

"Deepak, you are like my son. I have two sons of my own who are in America, and do not wish to join my firm. They have their own jobs, and they like the American way of living. In short, I have lost them to America." Tarachand ji's face showed his disappointment at the decision of his sons. He probably did not know how to mask his feelings, as Deepak read him well from his statements and from his body language. Deepak figured Tarachand ji to be a transparent person. He also felt it would be good to do business with the septuagenarian.

Tarachand ji continued, "I do not have a daughter. However, my business is generations old, and we have done very well over many centuries. We have created a seed fund and we could look at sponsoring your idea and taking it to execution." He looked at Deepak intently. Deepak felt it was a firm offer from Tarachand ji, judging by the way he spoke. Deepak knew he had an offer that could change the course of his life, his future, and give it an upward trajectory. Deepak knew in his mind that his father-in-law would advise him correctly whether or not to get into a business relationship with Tarachand ji. Deepak also felt that for a person of Tarachand ji's stature, his father-in-law would have no issues.

Tarachand ji saw Deepak mulling his proposal, and he knew in his heart Deepak was interested. It was his way, probably, into the big league. In Deepak he was looking for a bright young chap who could inject dynamism to his trade, something he so expected from his children, who were unavailable. He wanted Deepak's complete buy-in before they started the process. He said to Deepak, "Beta, I do not have a structure or the method by which it could work. However, I do have certain thoughts in my mind, and we could work on it if the plan even remotely interests you. I have also known your father-in-law for decades as we are from the same fraternity, and I am happy to meet Rajendra at his comfort, should it be necessary for you to take the discussion forward. I would also take some equity in the enterprise that we create, and have board seats arranged for my family. One thing is for sure, you would be the owner of the enterprise and that there would be no interference from the investor."

"What is the structure you are thinking of, sir? Why would you fund my idea? With your wealth, you could get a very good CEO to come in and manage your business while creating a new enterprise. So why me?"

"This question has an easy and an uncomplicated answer. You must understand the thought process of an investor. I am betting on you both as a person and as a businessman. I am putting my money on you," Tarachand said. He paused for a moment, and said, "We are facing serious trouble because of the governmental policies, and I am looking at a way out from the old way of thinking. I wish to inject new thoughts into the business, and appreciate the way you manage your father-in-law's business. You have ably supported your wife in her strategic decisions and in getting new contracts. A professional will not have an owners' mindset and enterprise. Beta, I like your hunger for growth, and a rare spark in your eyes for the trade. I believe that the structure would be equitable.

We could decide on a value which will get ascertained for you as a working partner and, simultaneously, if you were to bring in some seed money, that would buy you a portion of equity in the business. I want to do the detailed workings later, once you have further clarity on the proposal. I could put fifty lacs in the business, over a five-year period. So, if you were to bring in fifty lacs, then you would have a fifty-fifty partnership. Your sweat equity would be 5 per cent in the business. Are you in?"

"Yes sir. But unfortunately, I don't think I'll be able to invest anything at all. Moreover, I would also have to speak to my family, my wife, and my in-laws, before I could take a decision of working with you on your plan. So, please allow me some time."

"Sure beta. Take your time, and don't worry about the investment. We can take care of that later. So, beta, tell me, who else is there in your family?"

"Well sir, apart from my parents, there is my brother, Kul, and my wife, Guria. I know about yourself and your two sons. What about Mrs. Kajaria?"

"She is very much there. We are like two inseparable souls, and we have now been together for over forty years. Much alike your parents, only that they are younger. Alright beta, I am done here."

He invited Deepak over to his residence and to his office. He wanted Deepak to have a formal chat within his family. He also told Deepak that while he would be happy to co-create an enterprise together, but that should not be a consideration while Deepak thought this project through. He wanted Deepak to mull over it, speak to his family and to his immediate stakeholders, and then take a considered decision.

There were multiple thoughts running in Deepak's mind as he saw Tarachand off. He knew it could be a life changing event, but he had the responsibilities to grow his father-in-law's business too. Amit was not too well and Guria would be left alone if he ventured out for something big.

He knew he had to take it slow, consider the proposal in its entirety, and then take a call. It was not going to be easy, and so he decided to chew on it for a while.

Chapter 31
1976

"*Maulana* saheb, I don't understand why we are allowing the right-wing parties to join forces with us under Jan Sangh. Their agenda is completely different. A formation of the opposing forces would not go far. These disparate parties would explode, sooner rather than later. And whenever that happens, Jan Sangh will collapse. So why create a party that is doomed to fail?" the Shayar asked.

"I agree with you, but only partially. Jan Sangh may fail post-facto. However, this is being created with a different purpose. It will bring all the opposition parties together against the present-day government, and it won't allow any vote split amongst the different parties in the Opposition."

All the political forces in the Opposition were coming together, slowly but certainly, against the government of the day. They were prepared to give a tough fight to the party in power, during the elections, as and when it was called for. They wanted a two-party fight, akin to the Presidential form of government, like the USA. It was a fight between the haves and the have-nots. A fight between a united Opposition, against the might of the Ruling Party.

Maulana saheb said, "Once we have unseated the government and brought in a fundamental change in the polity of India, we should allow Jan Sangh to give way again to a multi-party democracy. See, our forefathers could have chosen the Presidential form of government."

With the benefit of hindsight, one can say that the country is better off without a two-party democracy. There is a good representation of all the religious and other groups in our polity. A judicious mix of the opposition parties was bound to ensure co-creating a fail-safe mechanism to take over governance. People in the country hoped JP could help the new government, whenever it came to power, to navigate the governance. The Press was bound by shackles and Indians were living their lives under a veil of secrecy which felt more like a borrowed life, than what they ought to have got after independence. People were not allowed to openly discuss normal politics in the country. The idea of India had taken a serious beating, and a lot of Indians were prepared to fight to get their beautiful and prosperous India back on track.

Maulana said, "Look, I may be a religious teacher, but I believe in prosperity for people in a democratic nation."

"I agree with your viewpoint, Maulana saheb. However, have you heard the cacophony of shrieks emanating from our slums? They are under great stress and their lives are at stake. They are worried for their safety in their own country. Why them, Maulana saheb?"

Maulana nodded, and said, "I feel petrified even at the thought of being whisked away for a forced sterilization. We have been reduced to the likes of animals. We do not have any voice left. This has shaken the confidence of the youth, and it is our duty to guide them out of this mess."

The Shayar interjected, saying, "And it is not only happening in Muslim slums, but in every slum now. So, it is not targeted against any religion, but against the poor of this country. It is against humanity, and we should give a fitting reply to it."

Maulana got a bit heated up in the debate and wondered why the government brought this forced sterilization agenda into their governance. He said, "The government created a thoroughly negative image for itself. Also, a complete ban of the freedom of the press went deeply against the government and its leaders. The government might as well realise that they have created a Frankenstein that they themselves don't know how to control."

The Shayar rubbed his nose rather brusquely, adjusting his glasses slightly lower on his nose, looking like a serious thought leader with greying hair and a polished disposition, and continued "We still get some information through our local political network, but a common man is denied it all. I'm thinking, can we create posters and banners with all the information at our disposal? We can hang them around or paste them across the city."

"Let us not take any hasty steps. We would have to seek approval from the party about this and take a call. But I don't think they will agree to this idea. There could be other ways of disseminating information, like through leaders of all the religions. Let us think it through."

"I agree with you Maulana saheb. Let me know what our role should be at this hour."

"I suggest you to create teams of six to eight volunteers and go to every slum around here. Educate them and manage their fears and expectations for a while. I shudder to think of it, but if there is a revolt of the masses, and if it is done in haste, it would go horribly wrong."

"With you, Maulana saheb. That kind of a hasty revolt will not last a day and it would be crushed with an iron hand. This government has shown its will, and we will fight against them to the finish.

"So, we must strategize and fight with our brains, for brawn will not win the day for us in this war. Peace be upon you!" Maulana concluded.

"Peace be upon you," Maulana saheb!"Farooqui returned.

Hope you understand that our countrymen were living in mortal fear. The situation was tense, and the citizens were not comfortable about their future. They could not plan anything in advance, and they had to live a day for a day.

Chapter 32

1976

"Babu, I wanted to speak to you privately. I need an hour of your time. Can we go to the veranda or your study?" Deepak asked.

"We can talk here also, Deepak. I don't think it will be a problem. Guria and Chitra are looking after the lunch preparations, so we can talk until they call us to eat. Chitra told me about the offer that someone has given you. Tell me, what have you thought?" Rajendra asked.

"Yes, Babu. I have met Tarachand Kajaria ji. He seems to know you."

"Yes, we are in the same business and his family has been in this trade for generations. They are decent people and good businessmen. Tell me, what did he ask of you?"

"He witnessed my short presentation at the committee meeting and then got in touch with me. In the meeting, I had spoken about the ability to earn better by creating a value addition to the products that we sell. Like selling branded dalia or atta, rather than raw products. That way, we could charge more and make better profits."

"I am aware, Deepak."

"He was impressed with the idea and he asked me to head a firm that would create a factory for any product or service that I would like to get into. He would fund it and give me a stake. There would be a working stake and monetary stake which, of course, I would have to invest for."

"Okay, that makes sense."

Deepak narrated his whole conversation with Tarachand ji while his father-in-law, Rajendra listened to him with rapt attention. He mulled over the shared information, and asked a question to Deepak, "What gave you the confidence to think that those branded products would do better. If you could back it up with some primary data, or at least some secondary data please. I want to know if you have spoken to any research agency yet, or it is still in the initial stages in your mind. Beta, I want you to activate a comprehensive qualitative and quantitative research on the subject, with a decent data size, and a pre-approved consumer base."

"I'll get the market research done. I'll also get the people to meet you so that you can approve of their methodology. I personally think that there is already a niche segment in the country which is ready for such innovative products. But let us not go by my hunch only. I'll commission this research immediately."

"You do that and then we can talk," Rajendra said and got up to go towards the powder room.

"But I still have a question. What if this research throws out pointers clearly indicating a market out there for these innovative products? Would you get into it yourself or would you allow me to go out and create this firm with Mr. Kajaria?"

"Son, you want to run a race, but business happens after much thought. If I do get positive indicators, I might want to get in myself. However, in that case, I may simply become Mr. Kajaria for you so that the business remains within the family."

"Well, that sounds interesting!"

"Else, I might buy a smaller stake and continue to help you increase your stake in the longer term to your commitment. So let us take it as it comes. We would convert it into action post the research. I hope I have been able to adequately take care of your concerns."

"Yes, Babu, completely. I should have spoken to you earlier. By now I could have at least commissioned the research."

"Don't worry, Deepak. You do not need to haste right now. All you require is a solid research and commitment to your dreams. It would soon get translated into action. I would recommend that you start working in the accounts section from tomorrow."

"Okay Babu, I will hand over my present marketing and sales responsibilities to one of my better team members. I need to learn accounting as well for running a business."

"Yes, it will be helpful in the long run."

Guria came in at that moment and said, "I hope both of you are done with your chat, because we would like to join in now."

"Guria beta, you could have sat through this conversation from the beginning. But don't worry, Deepak will bring you up to speed. Right, Deepak?"

"Of course, Babu. I would bring her up to speed later tonight. What is there for lunch today, Mumma?"

"Nothing much, *damaad ji*! We have *pulao, jeera rice,* aloo dum, kheer, *gatte ki sabzi, chutney, papad, achaar,* raita, and some sweets. We could not do much, given the time at our hand. If you had informed us of your visit this morning, I could have made *paneer ki sabzi* and some other dishes too. Anyway, let us go to the dining table," Chitra said.

"Oh my God! You have done so much already in so little time. We are in luck today!" Deepak said.

They were a happy family. Amit had begun investing his time productively in the business and he was once again positive about his life. He knew his parents would be able to get him married at the appropriate time. He had been able to remove all the negativity associated with his losing the ability to walk. He had taken it in his stride and had moved on. Deepak was a great addition to the family, while Rajendra was happy having found new friends in his life and elated as he was supposed to meet them soon.

Chapter 33
1976

Guria was waiting for Deepak in her bedroom. It was 11 pm already. They were generally together in their bedroom by 10 pm. Deepak was in the library. She had gone to get him over, but he had asked for about an hour more. The hour had passed. She could not sleep. She knew Deepak was working on the new project he had seemingly taken up. He was diligent and industrious. She wanted a bit more of him that evening, though, and she was wide awake. She thought about Deepak in her courtship days, and she felt orgasmic. He was the most trusted friend and the no-nonsense lover. He had taken care of her wishes even after their marriage. He did not touch her for over a week after marriage. He wanted to chat up with her every night they slept together, saying he wanted her to feel safe and happy together with him in their house. She had moved to his house, so he took extra care ensuring she felt good and happy. He would ask her a few times every evening if she needed anything at all, and if she was coping well with that massive change in her life, and she knew he was better than any other husband her parents or even God himself could have provided her.

She wanted him that evening. She needed to talk to him, as she wanted to understand his mental frame, and she could help him with his own feelings and counsel him thereof. She knew there could be no better mentor than her dad, but still she knew she could help him sort out his own problems for him, better than he could do himself.

Deepak walked into the room stealthily, making no noise, should he disturb Guria's sleep. However, he saw Guria looking at him with her dark, large, and beautiful eyes devouringly. She had shapely eyebrows, sharp nose, and an aquiline face that made her look like a diva. He felt an ache in his body, almost felt parched. He felt a longing for her body, that only she could quench. He walked up to the bed, stood beside her, bent down a bit, and kissed her on her forehead. She slapped him and pulled him beside her. He protested he wanted to brush, but his protests fell on deaf ears. She sucked his mouth almost feverishly, displaying a rare need to devour him that night. She wanted to be one with him truly, body and soul. One and whole, in unison, as the most beautiful creation of the world. Her body twisted around him, ripping his shirt apart, tearing over his jean in one swift movement of her hands, turning him over, and getting above him in a matter of seconds.

Deepak understood the cat was on a prowl and he had to commit himself to her need. Carnal desire had taken over and he went with the flow. He enjoyed the lead Guria took for the first time in so many days of their marriage. It was a genuine need in her that aroused him, and he started moving his hands and his lips in sync. He removed her gown slowly, sat up, and took her in his arms in a deep hug. She moved her manicured fingers on his back, scratching the surface with her multi-coloured painted nails, smothering him in her lust. He was deep into her that moment, and she pushed him down on the bed, moved her nails on his chest, on his belly button, kissed him there, and took him in her mouth. He understood the true meaning of ecstasy for the first time in his life, and his body moved with her, in tandem, in a simple harmonic motion till he came. They were drained of their living energy. Thankfully, Guria had kept a jar of cashew nuts on the bedside table. Both had cashews and then Deepak got up to brush. Guria went to the bath. While she was bathing, Deepak could see the charisma in her curves, the small love handles that she had, and he joined her in the bath. He used the loofa to give her a wonderful bath, dried her like a lover, and got her to her bed. She felt warm in the comforter, snuggled into Deepak's chest, and slept happily.

Deepak, however, could not sleep. He knew his brain was hyper-active, and he needed to do something about it. He had to think less, and probably work more. He had to work on his plan and make it foolproof. He had to get cracking on the research bit, do some independent study as well, and present the numbers in a presentable format to his father-in-law.

He thought of having a chat with his dad as well. Though he was a jailor, he knew his dad was intelligent and his insights were generally spot-on.

It was a lot of work ahead, and the national political climate was only deteriorating, so we still have to see if he was able to achieve what he set out to. I am sure you want to know too.

Chapter 34
1976

Deepak told his father-in-law Rajendra that he had given the research company a go-ahead on the plan. The plan was to conduct a thorough research for around two months and get back with their reports. They were tasked to conduct focus group interviews in eight different locations. They were to prepare a questionnaire, check in with Deepak, take his concurrence, and float it to their team in multiple locations to seek primary data points in large numbers. They were confident about getting at least fifty thousand responses, based on which they will share their market know-how. Meanwhile, Deepak updated Rajendra he was getting trained on voucher entry and other aspects of balance sheet and P&L accounts. Post that, the team would teach him money management.

"I hope to be up to speed within the next month or so. Thereafter, I would get into the purchase department and try to understand the important factors there," Deepak finally concluded his updates.

"Good! Ask *Munshi ji* to keep reporting to me on your growth in his department."

"Babu, Panditji was saying that he was coming to the office to meet you. I think he will be here anytime now."

"Yes, I know. Shayar Farooqui is also coming here. I will be busy through the day. Please ask everyone not to disturb me once my friends come here."

"Sure, Babu. I'll let everyone now."

"Also, please come in once after they arrive and say hi to Shayar Farooqui. He'll like that."

"Okay, I'll drop in for some time. Will get Guria along as well," Deepak said, and left.

Rajendra was working on an important agenda for the day when he saw Panditji, and the Shayar walk in. He got up to welcome them with open arms. As they got seated, one of the peons came in to serve them tea and snacks, and soon after Guria and Deepak too came into the room.

They exchanged pleasantries and thanked the Shayar for his lovely recitation during their wedding, before excusing themselves.

"It would have been great had the Professor also joined us here. I have not spoken to him ever since he went back after the wedding. Have you guys been in touch?" Rajendra asked.

"I spoke to him yesterday," the Shayar informed. He is good. He is presently taking tuitions and other assignments."

The Professor had not found a job till then, and he was somehow working tuitions to keep his engagement going and to keep funding his family's needs. However, he remained a committed solider against the Emergency. The Professor was of the opinion that *Bharat Mata* had lost her character and her future. And if he were to hold on to what he was doing protecting Bharat Mata in any way, it would still be a great contribution to nation building. He was also creating opinion against the Emergency and against the policies of the government in his own little way in the minds of his students.

Panditji said, "I had, in fact, spoken to the Professor just a week back. I had asked him whether he wished to shift to Patna and offered to help him find a good job here. But he wishes to stay with his larger family, at Ranchi. He said that as the times were tough, he must remain with his family. Moreover, their family had left Patna for Ranchi only a decade or so ago. So, they would not like to shift back anytime soon."

"So, only I have not spoken to the Professor. I will do so at the earliest, possibly tonight itself. Anyway, what is the political information that you guys are getting now?" Rajendra asked.

They discussed about the government of the day and its governance. Panditji said, "There is a power struggle going on in the top echelons of the government, not only amongst a clique of senior cabinet ministers, but also in the party's youth wing. Not all is as rosy as projected and there are many people within the Ruling Party who are unhappy with how things were going and were waiting for a chance to stab the government in its back. Moreover, the *Nasbandi* program has not helped the image of the government. Although it gave them a reputation of being able to implement their will, in a country like ours, it did not go down well with the common people. A big movement is going on against it and the undercurrent seemed to be quite dramatic."

"I agree with Panditji. I am working in many slums with a team of our committed soldiers. No one is happy. In fact, everyone is in a state of fear, and they do not like what they're seeing around them. They have multiple things to say against the administration. Even the Patna district administration is getting a lot of flak as they have started implementing the sterilization program in most of the slums. A lot of people have gone to their villages to avoid such actions. But how long will all this last is the question," the Shayar said.

They spoke about the political scenario and the future of the country till lunch and then again until teatime, after which they parted ways for the day. Rajendra was quite exhausted, and he went back home in the evening. They enjoyed their discussions, and their camaraderie grew. They had become almost akin to bosom friends, and such friendships at their age were rare. They also knew that it was rare, and they wished to keep it that way. They knew that it would take a lot of commitment from the four of them, but they were willing to walk the path. They were good family friends as well now, and they had decided to keep meeting up as family, whenever possible.

Things were heating up on the political scenario and people knew the tension would escalate. Common people bore the brunt of any such escalation, even if they were apolitical, and the country had probably seen the worst of such escalations, or had she?

Wish to know your thoughts on the increasingly politically motivated Shayar Farooqui, the life of the four families, and the price the country would demand of the four friends. Were they prepared to pay a price for the freedom of their country from the shackles of bondage and in favour of civil rights? Would Shayar Farooqui get more involved in the murky local politics and face the ire of the government? Think it through!

Chapter 35
1976

"Babu, I was thinking that we could discuss the report of the research agency and go through their findings about our proposed branded products. If you have a bit of time today, we can take it forward quickly," Deepak said, as he, Rajendra, Guria and Chitra were having tea.

"I have read the report, Deepak. They have done a great job. Their methodology was good and we must trust and accept their findings," Rajendra said.

"So, Babu, what should we do now?" Deepak enquired.

"We should do exactly what the document suggests. We need to get into forward integration in our agriculture business. It could be into production of sauces, atta, *maida*, *besan*, *sattu*, dalia, or anything else."

"Yes Babu, but whatever we choose, we should stick to that product or those two or three products for a couple of years and take it forward depending on the response from the market. I understand that we would have to invest a lot of money."

"It might need approximately one crore in capital expenditure and at least thirty odd lacs in a bank account to support the daily working capital. But we can get a working capital loan sanctioned and use it on a requirement basis. The question now is how would you like to create this firm? Would you want to work with Mr. Kajaria or you would want to do it internally amongst ourselves?"

"I think we should take Mr. Kajaria on board, with less than fifty per cent stake. We would keep fifty-five per cent. He would eventually reduce it to twenty-four odd per cent."

"That structuring can be done. So now that you wish to keep Mr. Kajaria involved, let us do it this way: we will give you five per cent as equity against your work. You would be involved in the business and will be the CEO. It will be your baby and you would run it the way you wish to. How much can you invest?"

"Well, I don't think I can invest anything more than one lakh right now, but you can continue to deduct any earnings that I may get over two years. We can freeze my investments over a two-year period, and you could allocate a share based on that. For example, I invest one lakh now and four lakhs over the next two years. So, I get a share equivalent to five per cent of the capital employed."

"I agree. We will speak to Mr. Kajaria and get him to agree to the same, so you reach ten per cent in two years.

I need to invest fifty lacs to take fifty per cent share, while Mr. Kajaria would have to invest forty-five lacs. I think he would be okay with that. This is workable. You can continue to increase your equity over the next three years." Rajendra said, in an animated fashion, beaming with energy, and with the sense of a bright future for the new business Deepak wished to create.

He continued, saying, "However, the hurdle rate might increase. We can discuss with Mr. Kajaria and let you know. Guria could also invest with you in your firm. That way you can increase your holdings quickly. What do you think, Guria?"

"Babu, I think you should give him ten per cent equity just for creating and managing the firm, apart from ideating in the first place. Anything less would not do justice. I have seen him work on it with a kind of passion only a few people possess, and I have no doubts that he will do a brilliant job. I'll invest as much as I can but will have to see what I can come up with," Guria said.

Chitra was smiling quietly.

"What happened, Mumma? Why are you giving your special smiles now? What did I do?" Guria asked.

"Nothing. I was just happy to see you put across your points to your Babu in favour of damaad ji. You are taking a stand in favour of your husband. It feels good to hear that."

"You know it's nothing like that, Mumma. I genuinely felt it and just spoke my mind. The rest is for the three of them to decide."

"I would be okay with ten per cent for Deepak, provided we are able to convince Mr. Kajaria. He is a shrewd businessman. Let's see how it goes. Why don't you set up a meeting with Mr. Kajaria, Deepak? We could meet any evening, starting tomorrow. Also, if you want the real equity that you wish to reach, you can borrow from me at a percentage lesser than bank rates. No one would give loans at a lower rate than that," Rajendra offered.

"That's very kind of you, Babu. But I don't think it'll be required. We should discuss our offer with Mr. Kajaria. Let's see how it goes," Deepak said, and got up.

"Yes. Call him up and let me know about the appointment. Also check if he would like to come to our office."

At that moment Amit came into the dining area on his wheelchair. He had a large smile pasted on his face which made Chitra glad.

"What's the matter, Amit? Do you have a girlfriend now?" she asked, with a wink.

"Why does it always have to be a girlfriend? Mumma? Can't I have a smile on my face due to any other reason?"

"You can and you must, beta. So, tell us what is it that has made you so happy? You must always share your happiness, so that it multiplies," Rajendra said.

"It's nothing much, Babu. I was just thinking that *di* and *jiju* should travel to Darjeeling. They need some time-off. Di keeps so busy these days and jiju is actively working on his own company formation. I like his idea, though. Are you investing in his company, Babu?" Amit asked.

"I am thinking about it, Amit. I am inclined to. We will meet Mr. Kajaria and take it forward."

"That would be great," Amit remarked.

"Babu, Mr. Kajaria is happy to meet us over the coming weekend, maybe Saturday at around three in our office. Should I confirm?" Deepak asked.

"Of course, Deepak. Please confirm. It would help us to take a decision and move forward with the project. Also, it would be great if you work on the capital expenditure a bit. We need hard numbers to discuss and finalise. Speak to some factory consultants and take some quotations," Rajendra suggested.

"Yes, Babu. Will do that," Deepak said.

"Deepak, the results of the focus group interviews were better as compared to the questionnaire. Why is that? What is their input on the same? I hope you have quizzed them about it."

"Yes, I have. The results were startling, as far as those twenty odd focus group interviews were concerned. They basically said that you have a better chance at explaining the concepts and due to the discussion, a better public opinion has been formulated. Discussion and debate help. Governments are thrown out using discussions and debates. However, in our polity of the day, there cannot be any discussion or any kind of debate. Even journalists do not wish to be quoted. The MISA law provides them enough bandwidth to harass and silence the protesters," Deepak said.

"Hold on here, son! Get out of your anti-government attitude. You would have to work very closely with the government, whichever one it is, to get your approvals. You would have to meet officials of various departments. You might have to meet a couple of ministers too. You must start visiting the Industries Department. I hope you understand. We are businessmen, and we must be on the right side of the government and carry out our work professionally. None of our personal biases should hold us back from exercising our *karma-dharma* and that is, increasing and prospering our business," Rajendra said, in a tutor-like tone.

"I agree with you, and I assure you that my political orientations would not come in our way. I promise that I will do everything necessary to create and run our business successfully."

"I need to meet a top guy in the Income Tax department as well. I need to check with him before putting up this factory of yours. We need to get an in-principal go-ahead from this senior chap. It is important and there should be no surprises on that count."

"I would love to come with you for that meeting, Babu."

"Yes, of course. Because at the end, it's you who will take the baton forward."

Chapter 36
1976

"Call Dhiraj," Dr. A. N. Sahay told one of the kids in the house.

After about five minutes the Professor walked into the room.

"Yes, *Babuji*. Did you call me?" he asked his father.

The Professor was completely enamoured by his father. He knew that his father would leave a legacy and it would be difficult to match up to his skills and his popularity. His father was known in the entire Bihar as not only an ex-Principal of law colleges, but also one of the best orators of the country, someone who had been given the Annie Besant Gold Medal for oratory, and someone whose oratory was known to have stung even the tallest of leaders with wit and sarcasm. The Professor, while he was a professor of English literature, knew he himself could never match up to his father's sharp memory, as his father could recite a Shakespearean play verbatim, page after page, on public demand, and even quote the page numbers. His father knew eight languages, amongst Urdu and Farsi, apart from having a flawless dialect in English and Hindi.

The Professor went to meet his father on being summoned.

"There is good news for you, beta. You would have known if you went to the college today."

"What is it, Babuji? Please tell me," the Professor said, impatiently.

"The University has agreed to re-instate you with your full seniority at Simdega College. It seems like you did very well at their viva-voce exams. I got to know that they were like students, trying to learn from you."

"Did I hear you right, Babuji? That is so great. You know literature is such a vast subject. If someone has read in-depth about even an era or a type of literature, any conversation on the subject could be dominated by that individual." The Professor immediately felt relaxed, sat down near his father, took the news in, and said with a beaming face, "What I did was smartly manoeuvre the direction of the interview. Thereafter, I had a field day. They did not know much about my subject, which has much to do with commonwealth literature. It felt like I was talking to absolute novices. I knew I had aced it."

"That is like my son! Never allow the opposition to wrest control, no matter what the situation is. If you show them a chink, they will pass an entire sword through it. Well done. I'm proud of you. So, when will you be joining?"

"Immediately. I was not doing much anyway. I just hope they give me a decent salary. We need to put the kids in school."

"Kids bring their own luck with them, Dhiraj! Do not worry! When success comes, it comes in a procession. My small advice to you is to keep away from any further agitations like seminars or discussions on the Emergency or the polity of India. Just keep away from all of this and earn a reputation in the Regional College. I have heard that the students there are way too naughty, and they hoot the teachers they don't like or agree with."

"Do not worry, Babuji. They have the voice of All India Radio to contend with," the Professor said.

"I know that Dhiraj. I am not worried. However, I repeat, stay away from politicking."

"Yes, Babuji. I know I will have to work hard to win back my reputation and my place in this world. I do not have anytime now for any childish talk on polity."

The Professor, like many others, had to get back to his life, pick up from where he had left in the past, and think about his own future, as also of his family. Times were changing, and he had to change. He could either completely give himself to the changing polity of India, join the opposing forces to the authoritarian regime; or get back to his life and to his pupils. He eventually chose his family and his students, over nudging the political debate in the democratic direction. He knew it was beyond him, and he was willing to consider the role of a Professor sincerely, and work towards the improvement of the life of his students, as also that of his family.

He assumed that the things would improve for him, for his family, and for his friends, but it was not to be.

Chapter 37
1976

Tarachand Kajaria entered Rajendra's chamber, carrying a walking stick in his hand. Rajendra immediately got up from his seat to greet the older gentleman. Tarachand was an elderly man who had earned quite a name as a trader in their community. He was an astute businessman, but he was known to be fair in their circle. Tarachand must have been a good-looking person in his youth, as he still maintained a decent figure, though he had lost his muscle mass. He was a rather tall person with light skin tone, and had a bit of hair on his ears, and some protruding from his nose. He wore thick glasses and walked with a limp. He generally wore a pure white kurta *pyjama*.

"Tarachand Babu, what an honour to have you at our office. I suppose I must have done something good to have you here," Rajendra said, effusively.

Right then Deepak walked into the chamber and greeted Mr. Kajaria.

"I don't know about you, Rajendra, but your *jamai* has already done something great at his young age. He is a brilliant boy and would go places in life. You too must be given credit for providing him with appropriate guidance without stifling his creativity and imagination."

There was a brief pause as a peon came in with snacks and tea, and after he left, Tarachand sat back in his chair, relaxed and ready for a long discussion.

"Tarachand Babu, how should we start the discussion? We know that you are interested in doing something together with Deepak. He is also quite keen. However, I also want to be a part of it. You see, he was helping us in our business here and he has got his entire training here."

"Rajendra ji, do not worry about that. Please tell me what the proposal is, and what gives you the confidence that his innovative ideas would be successful in this kind of an environment."

"We have got a complete market research done by a large research agency. They did twenty focus group interviews, and fifty thousand questionnaires were filled." Rajendra said with a booming voice. It showed his self-confidence and his faith in their research. He continued, "Here is the report. The findings are very clear. There is a need for this kind of products, but no one has thought about it yet. We would be the first in the business, so we can milk the market and grow it. Competition would come later. By that time, we would have taken out our capex and our advertising expenses. I am positive about the venture."

Tarachand cursorily read through the report, looked happy seemingly at what he saw, and said, "Okay, that's great. I can see that the survey agency has done fantastic work. So how do you propose to structure it?"

"We should give ten per cent to Deepak as the idea was his, and he would also be the working CEO of the company," Rajendra proposed. "Beyond that, he will invest one lakh rupees at present. We would allow him a time of two years to invest a further amount and every lakh would earn him a per cent in the company. That way, I guess, he would have five per cent of bought out equity in the company in two years. I would buy forty-five per cent equity today. You would buy forty per cent. We would allow Deepak to increase his stake over the next three years following the first two, by as much as he can. However, in the second round, every two lacs would buy him a per cent stake in the company. I hope that is okay with you, Deepak? I'm sorry I could not discuss it with you earlier. So, initially, I hold forty-five, you hold forty, and Deepak holds eleven. The rest four per cent would be bought by my daughter, Guria. Here she is."

At that point, Guria walked into the chamber and Rajendra introduced her to Tarachand.

"Guria, this is Tarachand Babu. You must have heard his name. He represents one of the oldest families in our trade in Patna. He is an honourable man and I have deep respect for him."

Guria touched Tarachand's feet and sought his blessings.

"Rajendra Babu, you are an amazing person. You have such a good understanding of this business yourself and are a self-made man. The respect is mutual. I agree to your proposal, and do not have anything to add further. Any exits of equity, however, would be mutual or at least on a first refusal basis. I hope you have figured out the exact investment and the working capital that'll be required. It is not a big deal though. Please get an agreement executed and a company formed. Deepak, I will share my chartered accountant's number with you. Go and meet him. Get it all organised. We should ink the deal as quickly as possible," Tarachand said, energetically.

The meeting was soon over, and all the parties involved were happy with its outcome. Tarachand and Rajendra hugged each other, before he blessed Deepak and Guria and left. Rajendra then asked the two of them to take an early off and the three went home together.

Chapter 38
1976

The Shayar and Panditji arrived at Rajendra's house and were greeted with tea and savouries. Their wives were shopping and were going to join them after a while.

"Have you guys heard about the forty-second amendment?" Panditji asked.

"Yes. So now we are Socialist, Secular, and Republic Nation. I think no one has a problem with being secular or republic. But what about socialist? Why tie us in knots with Russia or China?"

Panditji said, "I was a bit surprised too. What have they even given us? Are they better than Western European countries or America? Is American liberalism and market led economy bad for them?"

Rajendra said, "Well, let us not go there. It is a vast subject, and it would completely change the course of our discussion today. What we know is that the Constitution is being used to gain certain ends by the government. So, how does this help the government?"

"Well, it feels dramatic. It seems like Mrs. Gandhi, much like her father, has been a genuine student of Marx and Lenin. Even though India joined the Non-Aligned Movement, we never got any dividends out of it. In fact, because of that, America and the western world have become close to our foe, Pakistan," Panditji opined.

The Shayar carried the discussion forward with a nazm,

"Hamein Manzoor nahin yeh adayen teri,
Yeh dilkashi teri, Yeh bandagi teri;
Yeh badli hui rooh teri,
Tere dar pe khada ik musafir hoon main;
Gareeb hoon main, khudabaksh hoon main,
Maikhane mein mujhe bhi jagah de do;
Bhar bhar kar teri jholi mein humne votes daale hain,
Teri parastish ki hai, teri ibaadat ki hai;
Makkari se hamein kyon rusva karte ho?
Makkari se hamein kyon beparda karte ho?
Main khudabaksh hoon, gareeb hoon;
Mera saath doge bolte ho magar humse hi bair kyon karte ho?
Teri Aashiqui ka junoon kuch aisa hai
Ke aashiq ki hi tum dil-o-jaan se nasbandi karte ho,
Kahaan jayein aye maalik, ab tu hi bata
Kahaan jayein, hum kahaan?"

(I do not approve of your grace, of your style,
Of your beauty;
Of this changed soul of yours,
I am but a wanderer at your doorstep;
I am poor, I am a child of God;
Allow me some place inside your bar,
I have given you more votes than you could possibly count;
I have worshipped you; I have venerated you,
Why do you disgrace me with your craftiness;
Why do you unmask me with your guile?
While you say unequivocally that you would side with me, why do you work against my interests silently?
I am so madly in love with you,
But you get your beloved circumcised;
Where could I possibly go my God?
Where, where?)

"Shayar Farooqui, you have beautifully put your thoughts and your angst in a nazm. We are fortunate to listen to your couplets and *nazmein*. It's fantastic! Absolutely fantastic!" Panditji praised.

"If his immaculate and soulful poetry could be carried out in our newspapers or magazines, they would have created a revolution. His words have a strength that was not known earlier to me. Professor saheb also considers Shayar Farooqui as his own guru, his mentor," Rajendra said in his indomitable style, crushing his nose against his palms, sneezing simultaneously for effect and adjusting his position on his seat.

"Do you know you are a genius, Shayar Farooqui? I just hope you have kept all your work in a diary somewhere. We could contribute in the future to get your book out. It would be wonderful. It would heal so many souls," Panditji said, reverently.

Both of them looked at the Shayar with emotion, while Panditji got up and did some basic stretching exercises.

"I have my poetry and my shayari saved in a folder that I keep at my house. Najma is aware of my life's work. I know I write some stuff, but it is nothing like you gentlemen portray it to be. It is just ordinary stuff. There have been greats in the past, much better than me, and they also got published, like Ghalib, for example," the Shayar said, with a lot of humility.

"Janaab, *raham!* Raham!" Panditji exclaimed.

Rajendra and the Shayar shared a laugh among themselves at that.

"Please try some of these savouries before they go cold. I guess, you people have so much to talk about that nothing else seems important to you. I would nevertheless request you to talk about the good things in life, like poetry." Chitra came in with tea in a pot prepared in the quintessential style. She kept the pot on the centre table which was made of teak wood and had a veneer polish. There were carvings on the table. She poured tea in three ornate cups. She had prepared *kahwa* tea that evening. Everyone thanked her for her graciousness. She spoke again, "There is so much good to talk about, like life, business, arts, travel. Please discuss these things and not the present political climate of the country. It's just a request, for I don't want Amit to hear anything to do with politics right now. It is not good for him. I hope you understand and don't get me wrong."

"Of course! Of course, we understand. And we're also sorry if our conversation has caused you or Amit any strife," Panditji apologised. "We will not talk about it. Instead, we would speak about Professor saheb. I spoke to him yesterday evening and had a great news to share. He has joined the Regional College at Ranchi as a lecturer and has already started taking classes."

The Professor had a hectic life between family, friends and students. He was a hard-working professor who wished to see his students excel in their career ahead, and ofcourse in his subject. He would take extra classes for the weaker students. He was a social man, so he reserved some time from his daily schedule for his friends and colleagues. He planned to do some original research, so he was also pouring into a lot of fresh study material. He had a relatively large family back there, with almost twenty members, so that also took a bit of his personal time. He was never better, and he enjoyed himself thoroughly.

"For how many months could they have kept a person of his calibre out of work? He is smart and motivated," Rajendra said.

"He can easily control a large crowd of students. His voice is deep and loud, and he does not need a microphone to speak to even three hundred people at once. I had an opportunity once to listen to his recital of a Shakespearean prose. It was just a page, and out of any context. I could not believe my ears. It was so good, so engulfing. He is a gem, and I was always sure that he would find a job, no matter what. Let us celebrate his job and his persona! We are blessed to be his friends," the Shayar said, elated.

"We are all indeed blessed to be with one another. It is difficult to find real friends at our age. Most of the people we meet after growing up have their own agendas and interests in mind, and if not that, then they'd differ vastly from your thinking and worldview. Hence, it is very difficult to forge true friendships. We are, however, blessed that we found one another, and we should be grateful to the Almighty!" Panditji said.

"We agree with you wholeheartedly! We are blessed and we are together, and we would always remain so, both in our good and bad times," Rajendra said, and the other two concurred.

They chatted for some more time and then, as it got dark, left for their respective homes. Panditji dropped the Shayar at his place before heading to his own. When he got back, he found his wife waiting for him. She was dressed to kill, like she used to do years ago. That beautiful sight filled his heart with love and made his day.

Chapter 39
1976

Patna had seen intense action by the police and medical authorities in the slums surrounding it. No one was safe or sure in those days. People from all ages were being targeted by the authorities to fulfil their targets, and their incentives. It was a harrowing time for the common person as the protector had forgotten his duty or was asked to follow a different duty—probably, of oppressing people and ignoring the basic norms of civility and the right to life. While there was action in the streets of the city at odd hours, the outskirts of the city were punished randomly at any hour of the day. There was nothing humane about it and ridiculous targets were being followed to the tee. People were being forced at will to undergo vasectomy. At some times the force applied was money, as it is a powerful motivator for the poor, or at times the police baton. It was a sufficient motivator for those who did not fall for money.

The Shayar met Maulvi ji after completing his *namaz-e-jumma*.

He told Maulvi ji that he was going with a small group of their committed soldiers to the Patna City area which had some slums. The Shayar had received complaints from the locals about an increasing pushiness of the authorities. He felt that it was not right for the police to target certain sections of the society as they were poor and they were always at the receiving end of the injustices of the society, apart from the usual challenges they faced even from the elements of nature. He wished to create a notional boundary for the police, basically telling them to exercise restraint, as those poor people were supported by the intelligentsia, and they were not alone. He wanted the police to respect places and boundaries. He told Maulvi ji that he wanted to meet people in the local mosque there and educate them. He wished to go around the area in solidarity with the local populace."

"*Khuda aap ke saath rahein*! How many people are you taking there with you?"

"There are about twelve of us."

"I would suggest that you take at least twenty. This is no joke. The policemen of the area would realise you are not a local face in that vicinity. They may harm you if you are not adequately protected."

"Okay, Maulvi ji. I will go with a group of twenty *Mussalmans*. *Khuda Hafiz*!"

"Khuda Hafiz!"

The Shayar went in a small bus with twenty brothers of the same fraternity. They reached Patna City within an hour and the Shayar went directly inside the mosque. He met a large group of people there who were waiting to hear him. He made an aggressive rendition of his war cry and educated them to have faith in *Allah Tala*. He told them that all will be good, and things would change for the better. He gave them a lot of hope and happily distributed some blankets to the poorest of them. He also gave them his address and asked them to keep in touch, or if they were in any trouble. He said that he was also a common man, like them, but he would try his best to help them out and hinted that they should not be afraid of the police.

Having given them a lot of comfort, the Shayar came out of the mosque accompanied by a group of almost hundred people. He then started walking through the alleyways of the locality. People saw him and approved of him, for he had a presence that inspired confidence.

From a distance, a police Inspector was looking at the crowd. He asked his constable to find out who the man was and what he was doing there. The constable came back with the information that the man's name was Shayar Umar Farooqui, and he was leading the crowd.

The inspector, Nakul Bose, was furious. He said to the constable, "This Shayar is doing of a lot of things he should not be doing. I was the one who had put him behind bars the last time around. He was gone for a good three months. He was a novice then but now, it seems, he has become a bigshot political activist who has taken a hardening stance. We cannot allow that to happen. He is creating a simmering revolution here, and should be shown his place immediately, or else, he would turn the crowd against us in our own area. Call all the constables. Call the SI too. And bring the van. Let us take him for a circumcision today. *Mazaa aayega*!"

"I'll get the team within ten minutes, sir. Should we come here and get you or would you go directly to the site?" the Constable asked.

"I'll wait for you. We will go together."

The police van, as said, arrived within ten minutes and the team of policemen quickly moved towards the area where the rally was going on. They went silently, without their sirens on, and managed to surprise the crowds with their sudden appearance.

"Shayar Farooqui, *pehchana?* I'm Inspector Nakul Bose, your old nemesis. I had caught you the last time around. There was no Emergency back then, but you were behind bars for a long enough time. I thought you would have learned your lesson and become a changed man. And indeed, you have changed. But unfortunately, you have changed for the worse. You have become an active political opponent to the present administration, and you are coaxing people to disrupt the peace in this area."

"I'm doing nothing of that sort, Inspector Bose. I just came here to meet all these people. We are here only for religious work, and it has nothing to do with any political party. I am also not affiliated with any organisation that's banned by the government. So please allow me to move forward. We are a peace-loving people, and I was anyways going towards my car because I'm already late. I would leave for Patna right away. Thank you everyone. Khuda Hafiz! Peace be upon you, Inspector Bose!"

"Wait, don't run like this. You are a tall leader of the masses. There are so many followers of yours. I have heard that you were in Delhi during the Turkman Gate episode as well. You are a prized catch, aren't you? And so, we would take you with us to the station. I wish to speak to you about a few things," Nakul said, in a tone that was clearly hostile.

On cue, the other policemen started rounding up as many people as they could, and within a few minutes, they had rounded up at least forty people. They were then put in the van. Slowly the news spread in the area and a congregation of people started coming out of their houses, over to the street where the police was rounding up people. Police Inspector told his team to quickly evacuate from there as they could get in trouble. The Shayar was seated in the police jeep, along with the Inspector. He continued to plead with the Inspector to leave him and not to take him to the hospital. He was an old gentleman who never had a child, so sterilization operation did not make any sense in his case. The inspector had a mischievous smile and the Shayar understood that it was more of the Inspector getting back to him than a normal sterilization case. He was taken to a nearby hospital and the van followed.

The Shayar somehow convinced the Inspector to make one phone call. He called up Panditji and told him everything. Panditji asked him whether he was arrested or was he being taken for forced sterilization. The Shayar told him that he was unsure, but they had been brought to a nearby hospital. He said he was clueless and that he would plead with the Inspector. However, he requested Panditji to reach out to the police department and speak to the Inspector through someone higher up the ranks. Panditji promised his help and asked him to remain calm and strong.

Those were tough times for a common man. Panditji had spent so many years in the police department. He was a worried man. He wanted to save the Shayar by all his might. He dialled the Superintendent of police of the area and spoke to him asking for a personal favour. Would the Shayar be fortunate enough to receive the personal favour on time?

Chapter 40
1976

Panditji informed Najma and Rajendra about the detainment of the Shayar. He then contacted the Superintendent of Police for Patna City and spoke to him at length about the issue at hand. He explained to him that the Shayar was a good man, an upstanding citizen, and a fine artist. He was also childless as it is, then why on earth would someone want to sterilize him? The SP assured him that he would immediately send someone to the hospital and get the Shayar released.

Back at the hospital, Nakul Bose came up to the Shayar and said, "It is your turn now. Fifteen of your brothers have already been operated upon. Please move on to the operation theatre on your right."

"Please listen to me, Inspector Bose. I do not have any children even after thirty years of my marriage. How would it help you to send me under the scalpel? I am willing to go with you to your station and we can have a chat there. I just wanted to tell you that I am a God-fearing citizen, and I am a scholar. People meet me more for my ghazals, nazms, and shayari, than for any political agenda. I do not understand politics anyway. I just wish that everyone is happy, and no one is poor or suffering. Our government, I am sure, also wants the same. That is the reason why the forty-second amendment has been passed, making India a socialist country," the Shayar said, thinking that he needed to waste some more time before an order for his release could be sent to Inspector Bose from some higher up official.

Suddenly at that point, a Sub-Inspector came in looking for the inspector. Inspector Bose saw him and pushed the Shayar away from his sight. He then took Farooqui to the operation theatre himself, and asked the doctors there not to allow him to get out without the operation. The Shayar understood that there was a commotion happening outside and so he started screaming at the top of his voice. The Sub-Inspector came running in behind them but, by that time, the OT door had been closed, and Inspector Bose stood silently outside.

The Sub-Inspector asked him about the Shayar and informed him that SP saheb had asked him to be freed immediately. Inspector Bose told him that he was not detained but had been picked up with another forty odd people and all of them were undergoing the sterilization operation as per strict instructions from the higher authorities, and that the Shayar was already inside the OT.

The Sub-Inspector had been sent there specifically to stop the Shayar from getting operated upon but there was nothing much he could do. He saw a smirk on Inspector Bose's face and knew it was personal vendetta rather than an authorised operation. He went back thinking of reporting Inspector Nakul Bose's misdirected agenda.

The Shayar was brought out half an hour later, after being operated upon. He was asked to stay at the hospital for at least another hour, and then leave. He felt as though he had suddenly lost his voice and his intent to fight or question people. He felt listless and soulless.

"Shayar ji, I was here to meet you and to get you out even before the operation had begun. I was here upon clear instructions of our SP saheb. However, there was some commotion and by the time I figured out, you were already in the OT. I couldn't do much." The Shayar just nodded.

Panditji got to know from the SP that the operation could not be averted, but he was not being detained. He had been released and should be home any moment.

Panditji and Rajendra immediately went to the Shayar's house, but he was not back. It was late in the evening when finally, the Shayar returned. He was fidgety and was not able to stand properly. He saw his friends and instantly had a tear in his eyes, but he avoided their gaze and rushed to the washroom. A slow and excruciating half an hour passed before the Shayar came to the living room. Najma, who was deeply disturbed, had managed to make some tea and snacks for Rajendra and Panditji, despite their insistence to the contrary.

Farooqui sat on the sofa, opposite Panditji and next to Rajendra. He was silent and morose, and very much unlike his usual self.

Panditji told him that he had sent a Sub-Inspector with clear instructions from the SP. However, he apparently reached minutes late. Rajendra was rubbing his nose and his chin, quietly. He did not know how to speak to the Shayar, who had to undergo an operation that was totally unnecessary.

The Shayar only mentioned that the Sub-Inspector had come well in time. However, Inspector Nakul Bose had a personal vendetta against him, and he made sure that he was pushed inside the OT before the Sub-Inspector could even see him there. He thanked his friends for their help and for their deep concern before becoming quiet again. Panditji and Rajendra tried their best to speak to him and even humour him by broaching several topics of their common interests, but everything went in vain. the Shayar remained despondent and disinterested in any conversation, and so, after spending some more time with him and Najma, they said their goodbyes and left. But before leaving they requested Farooqui to remain in the house for a few days and not go out much. They also asked Najma to call them if any situation arose or anything was required.

Najma was naturally apprehensive. She had never seen her husband so listless and incapacitated. It was evident that more than the physical pain, it was the emotional trauma that was bothering him. He had been scarred mentally. Najma thought he would say a few of his couplets, even if just to vent out his own anger or grief, but he said nothing and went to bed straightaway.

Panditji, on their way back, called up the Patna City SP again and narrated the entire incident to him. He knew the SP wouldn't be able to do much, especially since now it was after-the-fact, but he felt it was an information against his junior that, as a supervisor, he should be aware of.

He also informed The Professor who became deeply disturbed upon learning of the incident from him. Panditji asked him not to worry too much and expressed a hope that the Shayar would soon recover from this trauma and regain his mental and physical balance. They knew that the Shayar they were friends with could not stay quiet for long and that with every little change or setback in his life, his shayari only improved.

Panditji also narrated the day's events to Anjana, and she was aghast at the treatment meted out to such a genuine soul.

The way the sterilisation program was being run was shocking to most people as more came into light following the Shayar's forced and unnecessary sterilisation. The next day a dharna was organised by almost five hundred people. They went to the District Magistrate's office and gave their representation. They spoke directly to the DM and requested the administration to sack Inspector Bose. They also demanded the administration to provide an official apology to the Shayar.

The DM retaliated saying that it was disgusting that it was being suggested that there was personal vendetta involved, rather than a pure and simple government program. He said he would check with the local administration and organise something soon. He, however, advised people to stay quiet and go back to their homes. He said he would not be able to stop the police from using their high-handed techniques or even arrests if they created an unnecessary agitation and advised the crowd to disperse and never get back again.

Maulvi ji, who was leading the crowd, knew that the DM would not do much. He thought of going to the press, but then also he knew nothing would happen. Their hands were also tied by the administration. The Emergency was a rare event in the affairs of the country, and it was fast turning out to be the darkest period of Indian history since independence. He hoped to see the same Shayar again. The Shayar who would rise like a Phoenix, and create many more heart-rending nazms. He wanted to see the Shayar back in his elements, talking philosophically, in his freestyle shayari.

Chapter 41

1976

"Panditji, sorry to disturb you, but the Shayar is not well. He is feeling some pain in the stomach near the groin and is very uncomfortable. I thought I would just check with you. Could it be an infection?" Najma said over the phone.

"Oh God, that's not good. Let me speak to my family doctor and get back to you." Panditji said with a deep discomfort in his voice.

"That would be helpful as the Shayar has always believed in naturopathy. But it would not be helpful in his present condition. Please note down the number and call me back here. I'll be waiting for your call."

"Do not worry, Najma ji. I'll do something immediately. Let me speak to my doctor."

Panditji rang up his family doctor and told him about Farooqui's condition. Upon receiving some advice from him, he promptly called Najma back.

"There is nothing to worry about, Najma ji," Panditji said in a soothing voice. "It could be a small infection. These hospitals that are being used for vasectomy operations are not usually clean and safe. So, there could be an infection, but it can be easily treated. I am sending an ambulance to your house immediately."

"Will you be coming over, Panditji?" Najma asked nervously. She was herself panting, talking quickly, and could be having a nervous breakdown.

Panditji said he would be positively there, probably before them, and counselled her not to bother much, but to prepare the Shayar so that he could go to the hospital. Ambulance was on its way while they spoke. Panditji had requested his doctor also to reach the hospital while he rushed there. The ambulance took the Shayar to the largest government hospital in Patna. Panditji was already waiting there with his family doctor, and the Shayar was immediately taken to an antechamber and examined. He was then asked to be admitted immediately. The doctor told Panditji that it would be better if he was there for at least a couple of days. The infection was spreading fast, and they needed to take care of it quickly.

Panditji relayed the information to Najma and told her that she would have a car to herself along with a driver. So, she needn't worry. He told her he was going back to office, but he would be back there that evening. Rajendra and his family members would also be there by then, so there was no need to worry. He assured her that the Shayar was in good hands and his family doctor would organise everything well.

Najma was happy that such quick action had been taken and she felt fortunate to have been blessed with such wonderful friends.

By the evening, all friends and their family members had gathered in the hospital. They were constantly checking with doctors if they needed any help. However, the news coming out from the ICU was not good. There was no improvement in his condition. The doctors were struggling and senior doctors had been sent by the administration on a mission mode mandate.

The news spread in the city slowly and enraged the common person. They were not happy at the turn of events, and they wanted the administration to do all it could to nurse back the Shayar to health. They demanded action from the district administration. A crowd slowly gathered outside the hospital, and they demanded Inspector Bose to be sacked immediately thereof. They demanded maximum care for the Shayar. Everyone had only a question in their minds, and they looked up for divine intervention. The Shayar was a man of God and people hoped he would get saved by providence, if not by doctors.

But were they sure?

Chapter 42
1976

Najma was worried. She did not go back home that night. She knew it was a tough night and she had to be there with her soulmate. The Shayar had been a good husband and she loved him. Her heart sank but she kept herself up all night. She kept sending the blessings of the Almighty to the Shayar. She was chanting constant prayers. Panditji and Rajendra were back with Najma in the morning. They were at least happy to know that the Shayar's condition had not turned worse from where he was a night earlier. That gave them faith. They felt the Shayar was fighting his winning battle against all odds.

Doctors came to Panditji after their morning rounds.

"We are sorry to tell you that the infection has spread into the other critical organs. So, while we do not wish to say it, but we feel the Shayar could be on his deathbed. We are doing all it takes to nurse him back to health."

Panditji felt heart-broken. He had sweat gush out on his temple. He wanted to ask something, but his voice gave in and he cried softly. The doctors held him and seated him in a nearby chair. They asked the nurse who was on rounds with them, to give Panditji a glass of water, and to inform the other family members to seek blessings for the Shayar. This news numbed everyone around. Najma was quiet. Others were as well. The news spread in the city like wildfire. People gathered to the streets and moved towards the hospital. Police presence was increased within the premises of the hospital and a major police posse was posted at the hospital gates. They had sensed trouble and put-up barricades and barriers up to five hundred metres from the hospital. Police presence was nudged up multiple notches across the city to prevent any major escalations with people, and also to save government property.

The DM knew people were deeply hurt and pained by the turn of events and they could take any step at that hour. Masses did not see reason during such congregations, and they knew various political parties had ignited the spark that might blow out the government. He was under strict orders from the government to get down heavily if required, to crush the seeds of freedom. Armoured vehicles also arrived, and Patna looked as though it was a war-torn city. Patna was known to be a city of culture and a city of knowledge. Battle tanks roared inside the city main roads as a show of strength. People were advised to go inside their houses and the local administration promulgated Section 144. People were advised not to remain in groups of more than three to four, and the police had work to do. The district administration hoped against hope that the Shayar would get back to life and get discharged sooner than later. Inspector Bose had been suspended forthwith, pending an enquiry that would get constituted later.

Police effectively disrupted the gatherings across the city, within a matter of an hour. Everyone waited with bated breath, and should things go worse for the Shayar, the common person wished to fight a pitched battle with the police. People hated what had happened to their motherland and they knew these atrocities on the poor would increase the decibel to unproportionate lengths for the government. They felt an end was near for the Emergency, and something better should emerge. They felt sad about the cost a democratic nation had to pay during the emergency. The government was fighting a losing battle.

Suddenly senior doctors came in a group and spoke to Najma. They were the bearers of the sad news that broke her from within. The Shayar was no more. He had suffered a multiple organ failure due to septic that had grown unabated since the vasectomy, infecting his entire body. Najma felt like she had lost her bearing that day. She had lost her very being and she fell unconscious. The Nurses attended to her. She cried hoarsely, and uncontrollably. Panditji and Rajendra sat down looking dull and morose. They felt they had lost their very own. It was painful.

Anjana and Chitra held Najma close to them and together they broke in tears for the Shayar. It took a while to register they would never hear him say his couplets again. People felt shocked and anguished when they heard the news. City felt gloomy that day. The commoner felt cheated and deeply hurt. The government that they had put into the office, had lost the reason to govern.

The Shayar's death had a devastating impact on the three friends, and consequently, it had a terrible effect on their four families. Everyone felt deeply hurt and upset that such a good soul had to go just because of an improperly done operation, which was not necessary at all.

The Shayar's body was taken to his house after a few hours, where it was to be kept for the day as Najma wanted to wait for the Professor's arrival as she knew that the Shayar was very fond of the professor and his soul would be at peace knowing that he was at his funeral.

There was an intense pressure on Najma to start the Shayar's *salat-al-janazah* as early as possible. It had been difficult to convince the local administration to allow the body to be sent to the Shayar's house. The administration did not wish to have an impending crisis on their hands, and they wanted the final procession to be conducted at the earliest. Some honourable men from the community met the DM and convinced him to hold off the funeral for a day. They committed to him that they would not allow miscreants to disturb the peace of the area. They only wished the Professor's presence before the final procession.

Najma was steadfast in her stance that the funeral would happen only after the arrival of the Professor. She bluntly asked the policemen if they would force his funeral too, the same way they had forced his operation. The police had no answers and listened silently to her rant as she termed them as killers and nincompoops.

As time passed in the day, a lot of important people made a beeline to see the Shayar one last time. The police had a huge task on their hands as they had to control over twenty thousand people that evening.

The next morning, Maulvi ji came to begin the salat-al-janazah, as more dignitaries and other important people kept filing in to pay their last respects. But the funeral proceeded only after the Professor arrived and met Najma. He shared his condolences with her, being heartbroken himself, and she told him that she wanted to wait so that he could pay his last respects to her husband.

The Professor joined the funeral procession along with Panditji, Rajendra, and Deepak, while Chitra and Anjana stayed with Najma to console her.

The procession was attended by a large crowd of people who had come on their own. It was not a Muslim or a Hindu crowd, but a crowd of the common man and woman, who were frustrated with the government, the administration, and the law enforcement and were protesting the dictatorial rule by attending the funeral of the man who had died fighting for their cause. The police found it extremely difficult to control the crowd, as there were thousands of people who wanted to touch the Shayar. They felt furious at the way the country was being governed and a volcano was waiting to erupt within them. The common man had been taking one injustice after another in his stride, but the time was near for retribution, and there was a silent yet simmering upheaval in the air.

The crowd thinned by three in the afternoon as the Shayar was respectfully buried amidst tears and cries of anguish from his friends and well-wishers. The Professor, Panditji, and Rajendra went back to the Shayar's house to meet Najma and stayed there through the evening along with Chitra and Anjana. The Professor asked Najma if she knew anything about the Shayar's pink file.

Najma knew about it, and she gave it to him in the presence of the other friends. The Professor said he would compile all his written poems and couplets and get it published as a single book. It would be their tribute to the Shayar. He also offered to take Najma back to Ranchi to stay with his family, but Najma refused the offer. However, she assured him that she would travel to Ranchi someday and visit him at his place.

She also said to Panditji and Rajendra, "Although I have had many people from my own community who wished to take care of her, you are my only family. I would continue to stay at the same house where I have lived for so long with the Shayar and I would meet you all often. I ask to be given some time and privacy, at least for a month, to mourn the loss of my dear husband."

It was a request that nobody could refuse, for after all, they all needed time to mourn the untimely demise of the Shayar.

Chapter 43
1976

"It feels sad to see Najma this way. She was a happy and content woman. The Shayar was her life. I could not even get myself to speak to her today. With time, things would get more difficult for her, so we must support her, as and when possible," Anjana said to the entire group of friends, once they were at her house.

"Absolutely! We will take care of her. She would be like our extended family, and we would involve her in every function and every party. She is one of us and she will continue to take part in all our future activities," Rajendra declared.

"There is no stress there, I guess. From my end, I speak to a couple of publishers. I may need your help there as most of the publishers are from Patna or Delhi. We need to get this book published as its royalties will go a long way in helping Najma with her daily expenses, now that the Shayar is no more," the Professor said.

"Yes, anytime. Just let us know who you are talking to, and we would do our best to chip in. It would also be a fitting tribute to the gentle person we knew as our friend and an extraordinary poet," Panditji said.

After a while, as they sat down for a late vegetarian dinner, the Professor asked, "Any fresh news, Panditji, from the political front?"

"Well, I have heard that there have been multiple cases of forced sterilizations across the country. There is a report of a forced sterilization of a man who was seventy-five years old and did not have any teeth or eyesight! There have also been forced sterilization-led looting and rioting by policemen in villages and *tehsils*. Recently, in Muzaffarnagar, police caught almost thirty people who were forced for sterilization, out of whom two were above seventy-five and two were under eighteen. Locals came in large numbers and demanded that the police release them. But the police opened fire and threw tear gas shells to disperse the crowd. Over thirty people died on the spot."

"This is a historic blunder that Mrs. Gandhi would have to share the blame for. It may have been carried out by rogue policemen, but the political price would be paid by the Congress party. No one else it going to take the blame anymore. It is a complete disaster in the making. Having lost the Shayar to one such rogue policeman, I feel ashamed and rather sad at the current situation," the Professor said in a slightly soft tone.

"It is going to be a silent new year. I do not see any revelry happening anywhere. We could spend the time together and have a quiet celebration amongst ourselves. That would possibly be the best way to end a gruelling and horrendous year," Chitra suggested.

"I agree with you, Chitra ji," the Professor said, then added, "I have a proposition. All of you please come over to Ranchi. The serenity and beauty of Netarhat is indescribable. The locals there are enterprising and they take care of the tourists well. They enchant their tourists to a brilliant local dance composition during evenings that everyone loves to watch. I suggest that the menfolk could go for some *shikar* as well. Upon the confirmation of everyone, I would book government-owned guest rooms in Netarhat immediately."

"That is a superb suggestion. We'll decide in a day or two and confirm to you, Professor saheb. Rajendra Babu, you must also think and confirm. This program can only be done together. I know that it is a beautiful location. There would be spine-chilling cold there during the year-end and we might spot some wild animals too," Panditji summed up.

"Yes, it would be good to take a break. All of us could go there and take the kids along as well. I think we should also take Najma with us, provided she agrees to it," Anjana said.

"Okay, so we need to think it through and take a call quickly. Speak to the kids today itself and let us come to a decision preferably by tomorrow. Would that be okay, Professor saheb?" Rajendra asked.

"Absolutely. And yes, the quicker the better. Government guest houses are generally not many in number and there is usually a beeline of tourists at Netarhat during the winters. I guess we would be okay if we can come to a decision by tomorrow morning."

The four families wished to take a break from their routine as they had never taken a break before as families and as friends. They would miss the Shayar, but they made it a point to include Najma in all their plans. It was good for Najma also to be a part of the group as she knew the Shayar would have wanted that as well.

Chapter 44

1976

Rajendra, Panditji, their families, and Najma arrived at Ranchi station as per their plan to go to Netarhat. The Professor was happy to receive them, and he proposed they go to his house at Bariatu Housing Colony. They could take a bath, have a decent breakfast, and leave for Netarhat. It was a journey of at least six hours by car, so it was a good plan, and while everyone considered the plan, Nilima said, "We cannot allow them to go directly to Netarhat. We must go to our house, get ready, and then leave. That would be the better option. Please come, all of you. The minibus is outside. It would not be much of a detour anyway."

Everyone got into the bus and went to the Professor's joint-family house, where they were lovingly welcomed. It was a very cold day and so they were immediately served tea and biscuits, and then were given hot water in tubs so that they could quickly take bath and get ready. After taking their baths, they were served a heavy breakfast and then, about an hour and half later, they were finally ready for the trip ahead.

The Professor introduced everyone to his father and his brothers upon their arrival.

"Dr. Sahay," he said. "You might not remember me, but I used to come to your home as a teenager in the Kankarbagh area of Patna. My elder brother, Sameer Agarwal, was one of your bright and most obedient students. He had taken law for his Bachelors and later became a famous lawyer in Patna."

"Oh wow! What a coincidence. The earth is indeed round. After all these years, I have someone here who remembers coming to my house as a teenager. Where is your brother now? I knew him well and he used to meet me frequently when I was in Patna," Dr. Sahay enquired.

"He is no more. He was the lawyer in the news a couple of years ago when he suffered a heart attack inside the court premises while defending one of his clients," Rajendra informed with a slight lump in his throat.

"Yes, I remember hearing about it but had no idea it was the same Sameer Agarwal. What a pity. He was a great boy. See, Dhiraj beta, we are all connected by an old thread. Your friend's elder brother was one of my better students and he went on to become a celebrated lawyer. He was one of his kind in Patna and had won some of the toughest of cases for his clients," Dr. Sahay said.

"Yes, that is not surprising to hear, Babuji! All the judges and lawyers of Patna High Court and the local courts and quite a few judges of the Supreme Court have been your students. What is good to know here is that Rajendra ji used to come to our house. So, I would request you, Rajendra ji, to feel at home and be the host to the travelling team here."

"I have very fond memories of a few of my visits to your place, Dr. Sahay. I was never interested in the English language or law. I was always into commerce and business. However, you used to speak to me at times and tell me the tales of achievers from far and beyond. You were the first person to have told me to fight for my rights and to create my own path under the sun. You told me to be the best in whatever I wanted to do. I am happy to tell you, Dr. Sahay, that I have created an agriculture trading firm all on my own and now it is well established. Thank you for being the sole motivator to a teenager."

"Those were different times, Rajendra. Nowadays it is difficult to even talk straight to kids. They are always in a hurry. They might respect you and listen to you, but they will not follow you. Anyway, I've taken up a lot of your time. You guys should be on your way now. It would take a couple of hours to reach Netarhat. All the best," Dr. Sahay said and bade them goodbye.

They left for Netarhat at ten in the morning and reached at around four in the afternoon. The guest house rooms were already booked in advance and a dual menu of vegetarian and non-vegetarian fare was ready for lunch when they arrived.

They directly went towards the sunset point. The scenery was beautiful, but the terrain was difficult. There were forests all around and even this late in the afternoon, they could clearly hear the sounds of a variety of animal species.

They witnessed a beautiful and breath-taking sunset, had some warm tea at a local stall as it was freezing there, and then they checked-in at the guest house just after dark. The guest house manager had advised them not to remain outside during the night-time and had suggested that they do their sightseeing from early morning till dusk, when there would be light and therefore would be a lot safer.

After freshening up, the entire group converged in the living room of the guest house accompanied by snacks like egg-devil, onion pakora, and lots of tea and coffee, the conversations flowed. The ladies talked amongst themselves while Deepak, Guria, Kul, and Amit formed their own group, and the three men sat together on the sofa opposite to them and spoke between themselves.

"This is a beautiful place. Can you tell us a little about the geography and the flora and fauna of this place, Professor saheb?" Panditji asked.

"Certainly. Netarhat is at thirty-five hundred feet above the sea level. This hill station is also called the Queen of Chhotanagpur. It is in the Palamu district of Bihar. Tomorrow we can go and see the Netarhat Residential

School. It was set up in the early fifties and, I don't know whether you are aware of it or not, it is possibly one of the only *gurukul* learning based schools left now in the country. The school graduates are some of the brightest kids of the country year after year."

He continued, "Netarhat is a plateau of approximately only six kilometres by four kilometres and it was covered on all sides by lush green forests. It has pine trees, pear trees, sal, mohua, kendu, and eucalyptus. One can find a lot of animals and birds there and just about sixty kilometres away was the first wolf-protection sanctuary of India. Actually, this year itself, on twenty-third June, the wolf sanctuary was created in Mahuadanr. There are multiple waterfalls in the area and we could go to a couple of them next morning. In the afternoon, we could go to the interiors a little with those airguns." The Professor was carrying two guns.

"What do you guys say? An adventure, anyone?" The Professor looked expectantly at the other two.

Rajendra and Panditji, however, were not too hot on the idea. They thought it might not be wise to go deep into the forest, especially since they had already heard animal cries emanating from the jungles and had no qualms in admitting that they were scared, despite the presence of guns. The guest house though was safe, but the manager had still advised them to stuff in newspapers in the crack of their doors to prevent snakes or any kind of insects from sneaking in. It was also a way to keep animal sounds softer and quieter.

It was quite an evening. The Professor regaled the group with his stories of Simdega and Kahalgaon where he used to stay earlier. He narrated how he used to cross the Ganges on a hired boat along with a couple of his friends, go deep into the jungle, and kill *chaha, teetar,* and *bater* with his airgun.

At around nine, they had their dinner, and post it, they again sat down in the living room for a while and Panditji requested Nilima to sing a couple of songs of her choice. Nilima obliged after some initial hesitation, and sang a couple of Lata Mangeshkar melodies. Then, around ten-thirty, all of them finally retired to their rooms. They did not believe in ringing in the new year at midnight. They rather believed in getting up early on the new year day and meeting everyone with heart-felt greetings.

The first day of their vacation was over and they were looking forward to an even more adventurous time the next day. But amidst all of it, somewhere deep in their hearts, each of them missed the Shayar and felt bad for Najma and her loneliness. There was only one question in their minds—could they still have a nice vacation and have happy memories for the rest of their lives?

Chapter 45

1977

The group was at the sunrise point just as the sun was making its grand appearance for the day. New year vibes were already in the air and even strangers were wishing one another. There was an unshakable hope in everyone's hearts that the dark period of the Emergency would soon be over and that they would see a healthy and just democracy once again.

The scenery in front of them was mind-boggling. The sun was a mesmerising ball of fire which became brighter as it rose from below the horizon into a pale orange sky. It had been a chilly winter morning with the temperature dropping well below normal, and the sunrise finally brought along with it some much needed warmth. After seeing the sunrise, the group had a cup of steaming tea each from a local vendor. Warm and rejuvenated, the group went ahead for the site visits planned for the day.

They reached the Upper Ghaghri falls within half an hour around five thirty. It was just below the Netarhat dam, and the sight was picturesque. The cascading water dropping from over three hundred feet made sounds that were soulful and intimidating at the same time and they also had a serene calming effect on their minds. Nature was bigger and humans were inconsequential in the larger scheme of things. The realisation happened to the group, and they thought about the Shayar, about the couplets he would have created watching the ethereal beauty of the waterfall, and moved forward towards the dam.

It was quite a large dam with an expanse of four-square kilometre and was filled with delectable varieties of fish like *rui, katla, mrigal,* etc. The place was for a picnic or just for relaxation and, being that early in the morning, the quietness of the place was intoxicating.

From there they moved towards the Lodh Falls. It was the highest waterfall of Bihar and while they were there, they wished to see it for themselves.

When they reached it, around eight in the morning, they could hear the waterfall from a distance. It took them some effort to reach a proper vantage point for viewing the gigantic falls, as there was a thick forest cover around the area, and they were afraid of the likely presence of animals and snakes, as the Betla Forest was nearby. They eventually managed to find a good spot.

The beauty of the waterfall was mesmerising. A gigantic gush of frothing water was cascading down from a height of almost five hundred feet. It felt like time stood still. The entire area had a high humidity level and with such low temperatures, one needed tea at frequent intervals. It was good that they had taken a flask full of tea from the teashop at sunrise point. Women held their men romantically watching the cascade, and soon they realised Najma watching the scene alone, with a tear in her eye. Nilima embraced Najma and made sure she felt loved in the company of her best friends.

All of them sipped tea and had some basic snacks like bread and butter there in a small picnic like setting. But the air was ravenous, and they needed a proper breakfast. There were only two options in front of them—go to a nearby tribal village for food or return to Netarhat. They chose the latter option.

It took them almost two hours on the way back as there was some traffic, and it was past eleven when they finally got back. They found a small *dhaba* and ordered a hearty brunch for themselves.

Next, they went to the Koel viewpoint. It was supposedly the most romantic place in Netarhat where one had a view of the Koel River flowing through the valley with pine trees on either side. It was surreal. They stayed there for a while and wished that the Shayar too had been there with them. He surely would have dedicated a couplet or a nazm to the locales.

Finally, they decided to walk through the pine forest near their guest house, an exercise of an hour or so, before heading back for lunch. It was a long romantic walk, made more enchanting by the windy and cold climate, and they were glad that they came here and left their footprints on the sands of time.

Back at the guest house, they played cards and other board games which extended till early evening, by which time they had enough tea to ward off the cold. The blower was working its magic, and the togetherness they felt within the group felt like a gift given to each of them by a higher power. Soon it was time for dinner, and they found a lavish spread waiting for them at the table. After a hearty dinner, filled with much laughter and banter, they decided to call it a day around nine. They had to leave for Ranchi early the following morning to catch the evening train to Patna.

They left for Ranchi around ten the next day after having a heavy breakfast to keep them filled for the next few hours. The Professor had informed his folks back at Bariatu to keep lunch ready for the entire troupe, and so when they returned at around two in the afternoon, a hot and fulfilling lunch was waiting for them.

Then they had a *goshti* there as well over tea and snacks. There were many kids in the Sahay household and all of them got along with the group in a way that didn't feel like they were meeting them for the first time.

Chitra and Anjana too loved the company of Nilima and the other ladies of the family. Najma was quiet at times, perhaps imagining how it would have been had the

Shayar also been there, but overall, she managed to keep herself as cheerful and involved in the conversations as possible. She felt deeply thankful to her late husband for finding her such amazing friends for without them, her life would have been quite a drab and lonely, especially now after his demise.

Epilogue

1977

People were out on the streets in every single town and city of the country. The government had called for fresh elections to be held in the month of March and all the political prisoners were being released.

For the common populace, it came as a massive relief. It was a big day for the country, and the people could not believe it to be true. They had expected the Emergency to be called off soon, and for a while now it had only been a question of when. They also knew that along with the Emergency, the high-handedness of the police would also end. There was light at the end of the tunnel. Over one lakh political prisoners were released from various jails across the country and some of them, like Arun Jaitley, had spent a long time behind bars after having been arrested during the start of the Emergency.

Deepak was on track to creating his own firm with an equity partnership between him, his wife, his father-in-law, and Mr. Kajaria. He was happy at the way things had turned out for him. Their agriculture trading business had taken off as their margins started to improve. Deepak had big dreams from a new, post-Emergency India. He wanted to make it big by creating a large brand and he wanted to come out with an IPO within the first three years of setting up his plant. He was already thinking of a new and powerful India without much corruption and a newfound energy within the government as well.

Deepak felt that the newly elected government, which was to take charge by March end, would take all the right steps to take India on the path to glory. The country's destiny needed to be written by youngsters like him and so with a glint in his eyes, he set out on his path.

Panditji was a happy man. His jail had suddenly seen a reduction of prisoners by more than seventy-five percent. His staff had been overstretched during the Emergency and so he now felt that he could give some breather to his colleagues. Those had been a tough two odd years, and he was proud to have managed his prison quite well all this time.

He also knew that Deepak was on his way to creating something big of his own, and he was glad that Rajendra was there to guide him through it. He had enough confidence on Deepak and his ability to create a good organisation and was sure that his son would make it big. Both he and Anjana were also happy about the fact that Kul had also begun taking interest in important matters at home. He was getting more involved with the decision making in the family and was actively participating in most of the discussions.

Rajendra too was happy at the way things had ultimately panned out. He knew in his heart, or he wished to believe, that the present government would be badly defeated in the ensuing elections and a new government will be formed, becoming the first non-Congress government of the country. It gave him immense pleasure to think that he was also a part of the movement against the Emergency and the autocratic handling of governance. He was extremely proud of Amit, who had taken part in similar protests which ultimately, and quite unfortunately, led to him being confined to a wheelchair.

He was also supremely proud of both Guria and Deepak. While Guria was proving herself to be an able administrator, learning the ropes of being a good businesswoman fast, Deepak had emerged as someone with a shrewd business brain, an incomparable aptitude for knowledge, and a hunger for growth. Rajendra knew that because Deepak had ventured out on his own. Meanwhile, the future of his business rested upon the shoulders of Guria and Amit, so he had taken it upon himself to train them as well as he could to be prepared for the many challenges that they would inevitably face moving forward.

With the business slowly being passed over to the next generation, he and Chitra had a lot more time together and they spent it by socialising and attending various events apart from finding a newfound interest in each other.

Najma had become almost a weekly visitor to both theirs and Panditji's homes, and they made it a point to include her in all their social gatherings. She was extremely happy and excited as the Professor had been able to get the Shayar's book, including almost three hundred couplets and nazms, published. Furthermore, apart from Urdu, the book was being published in English and Hindi as well. They had had a small launch for it, and it instantly become a bestseller, selling out the initially printed thousand copies and forcing the publisher to order for another ten thousand copies. It also received rave reviews, with praise being directed to the Shayar's deep thoughts and flowery prose. The Shayar had become a sort of a cult hero to the faceless masses for the way he had fought for them and gave his life for the cause. So, the people wanted to buy and support his book as much for honouring him as well as for reading his beautiful verses.

Najma knew that it was a gift that the three friends had given her and all the monetary compensation coming in from the sales of the book was more than welcome in her situation. She was a lady with a high level of self-respect, and she wanted to be able to live happily within her own means. All that the Shayar had left for her might not have carried her for more than a couple of years. But through the royalty of his book, she would be able to live her life quite comfortably.

The Professor was doing well at his college, and he had regained all his lost respect and credibility. His students loved him and admired his style of teaching. He incorporated an element of drama in his lectures, making his classes not only informative but entertaining as well. The performance of all the students in his subjects had seen a vast improvement since he had taken over, and his success was not lost on his seniors or the head of his department.

The Professor had a busy and happening life outside his college too. He had become a renowned speaker at Ranchi, and he was constantly invited as an honoured guest in many functions. He contemplated jumping into the political scene himself officially but was advised against it by his father.

So, he mulled the option of getting himself a PhD. He knew it would take a lot of time as it would have to be done with solid research. He decided to have a chat with Nilima about it too, as he was aware that it would mean a lot less time for his family for a long period of four years.

Nilima was happy in her life as a housewife and she looked after the entire extended Sahay family along with her sister-in-law. Nilima and the Professor's kids were admitted to reputed English medium schools and were being brought up in the best manner possible. The kids had already started showing amazing results and a great aptitude not only for studies, but in other extracurricular activities as well, with the girl showing a penchant for poetry that she would keep reciting endlessly throughout the day. Dr. A. N. Sahay loved listening to her for hours and invariably spent time with her after wrapping up his engagements for the day.

The mood throughout India was positive. The people had clearly expressed their disdain for the Emergency and welcomed the decision to call for elections with open arms. The masses were elated at the turn of events and felt that the dark days were finally over. It was time to rejoice and start afresh. The Emergency, likely, was to be lifted soon, and the people's voice and their decision were about to get reflected in the ballots.

The rest, as they say, is history!

Glossary

Aloo dum	A North Indian dish where baby potatoes are steam cooked in a delicious gravy.
Achaar	Pickle.
Adab arz hai	To offer respect.
Allah tala	The Almighty.
Antakshari	An Indian singing game where you sing a song using the last letter of the song sung by the previous person/group.
Arz kiya hai	I propose to say.
Atta	Flour.
Begum	A married Muslim woman.
Besan	Chickpea flour.
Bhajan Sandhya	An evening of singing devotional songs in Hindi.

Bhava	The emotional or devotional state of a person towards a particular deity, concept, or spiritual goal.
Brahmin	The priestly caste in Hinduism.
Chaha, Teetar, and Bater	Different types of birds.
Chandaal Chowkdi	A group of miscreants.
Chulha	Gas burner.
Chutney	A thick sauce of Indian origin used as a condiment.
Dalia	Cracked wheat.
Dhaba	A roadside food stall or restaurant.
Dharma	Dharma in Hinduism means religion, virtue, duty, and morality.
Dosa	A type of thin pancake made with crushed lentils and rice, originally from Southern India.
Garibi Hatao	Eradicate poverty.
Gatte ki Sabji	A traditional Rajasthani curry dish made with chickpea flour sausages cooked in a spicy yogurt based gravy.
Ghat	A flight of passages on the river-bank leading to a river.

Ghazals	An ancient form of poetic expression originating in Arabic poetry, written in the form of multiple two-line couplets following a particular rhyming pattern of AA, BA, CA, DA, EA, etc.
Gheraod	Encirclement usually by activists.
Goshti	A meeting in a small group.
Granthas	Religious or sacred texts in Hinduism.
Gurukul	A traditional method of teaching that was practised in India for centuries. It literally means "home of the guru," and it refers to a type of school where students live and study with their teacher in a residential setting.
Harijans	Translates to "Children of God". It was a term used by Mohandas Gandhi to refer to the community of Dalits.
Jamai	Son-in-law.
Janab	Janab, Janaab or Janob (Persian spelling) is an Islamic honorary title, which means "Sir" in English.

Jeera Rice	Cumin rice.
Jihva	Tongue.
Kaala Paani	The Cellular Jail, also known as Kālā Pānī (literally, "Black Water") was a British colonial prison in the Andaman and Nicobar Islands. The prison was used by the colonial government of India for the purpose of exiling criminals and political prisoners.
Kahwa	Kahwa is an exotic mix of Kashmiri green tea leaves, whole spices, nuts and saffron, which was traditionally prepared in a brass kettle known as samovar.
Kalyug	Kaliyuga in Hindu mythology, the fourth (present) age of the world, characterised by total decadence.
Kamardhani	A belly chain or waist chain worn by women in India.
Karma	The word karma comes from the Sanskrit word for 'work' or 'action'. It means that a person's actions determine whether good or bad things will happen during this life cycle and in the next.

Karmic	Karmic means related to deeds. For example, Vedic astrology emphasises the role of "karma" (deeds) of present and past lives on the health of a person.
Kheer	A sweet rice pudding cooked in India.
Khuda apke saath rahe	May God be with you.
Khuda hafiz	May God be your guardian.
Kranti	Revolution.
Kurta Pyjama	Originating from the Urdu and Persian words, "Kurtah" means a loose-fitted collarless shirt and "Pyjama" or "Pay-jama" means clothing for legs.
Lathi	A long-heavy bamboo stick used by the Indian police.
Lehengas	A full ankle-length skirt worn by Indian women usually for a ceremonial occasion.
Litti chokha	Litti is a main-course dish that forms a part of the Bihari cuisine. It is a wheat flour cake filled with fried gram flour, that has been salted and baked. It is served with mashed potatoes and mashed brinjals.

Maharaja	Emperor.
Maida	Refined wheat flour.
Mandap	A temporary platform set up for weddings.
Marwari	Any of an Indian ethnic group originating from the Rajasthan region of India.
Maulvis	A learned teacher or doctor of the Islamic law.
Mazaa ayega	It will be fun.
Memsaab	Madam.
Miya	A Muslim title of respect like "sir".
Mussalmans	Muslims.
Naan	A round, flat leavened bread that people eat in the Indian subcontinent.
Namaskar	An Indian way of greeting.
Namaz-e-jumma	The jum'ah, which replaces the usual noon ritual prayer, must take place before a sizable number of Muslims in one central mosque in every locality. The obligation of communal worship on Friday is enjoined upon Muslims in the Quran (62:9).

Nasbandi	Sterilisation, vasectomy or tubal ligation.
Nazmein	Poetry, verse, string, order in Urdu.
Nirvana	A place of perfect peace like heaven.
Paan masala	A herb, nut, and seed mixture that is commonly served in India. Pan Masala is most often considered to be an item to aid digestion or used as a breath freshener for use after consuming highly spicy meals.
Pagdi	Turban.
Pagli Ghanti	A specific type of bell sound used in Indian prisons that tell prisoners and the police there's something wrong in the prison premises. It is assumed that prisoners would run towards their cells as soon as they hear this bell.
Pakoras	A fritter originating from India.
Panditji	A teacher or wise man, the word is also used for Brahmins in Hinduism.
Paneer ki Sabzi	A curry dish made from cottage cheese in India.

Papad	A dough of black gram bean flour is either deep fried or cooked with dry heat (flipped over an open flame) until crunchy.
Pehchana	To identify.
Pista kulfi	A frozen dairy dessert made using pistachio, originating from the Indian subcontinent. It is often described as "traditional Indian ice cream".
Poori	A deep-fried bread, made from unleavened whole-wheat flour, originating from the Indian subcontinent.
Pujas	Worship.
Pujya pitaji	Respected father.
Pulao	A popular rice dish consumed in the Indian subcontinent, and the Middle East.
Raham	Mercy.
Raita	An Indian side-dish, made with yoghurt, seasonings and diced cucumber.
Rangarang Karyakram	A variety program in the Indian context.

Rasa	Rasa, (Sanskrit: "essence," "taste," or "flavour," literally "sap" or "juice") is an Indian concept of aesthetic flavour. It is an essential element of any work of visual, literary, or performing art that can only be suggested, not described.
Roti, Kapda, aur Makaan	Literally translating to "food, clothes, and shelter", often used in the context of poverty in India.
Rui, Katla, Mrigal	Different types of fish consumed in India.
Salat-al-janazah	A funeral prayer of the Muslims offered with the participants standing and with the body of the deceased placed in front of them.
Salwar kameez	The outfit comprising of a pair of trousers (salwar) and a tunic (kameez) that is usually paired with a scarf (dupatta).
Samdhi	Father of the child's spouse.
Sampoorna	Complete.
Sampoorna Swaraj	Complete independence.
Sangeet	A musical night of partying during an Indian wedding. It also translates to "music".

Sarasvati Maa	A Hindu goddess who represents education, creativity, and music.
Sari	A garment worn by Hindu women, a long cloth wrapped round the waist and passed over the shoulder.
Sattu	Roasted gram flour.
Shayar	An Urdu poet.
Sher O Shayari	A pair of verse lines in Hindi or Urdu; couplets.
Shikar	Hunting.
Swarajya	Self-governance, independence.
Tasleem	Urdu form of greeting, salutation and submission.
Tehsils	An administrative area in parts of India.
Vignaharta	A destroyer of obstacles, Lord Ganesh.
Zanjeer	Literally translating to, "shackles and chains". Also a 1973 Indian movie starring Amitabh Bachchan.

Acknowledgements

I want to express my heartfelt appreciation to those who have made this project a success. Without their unwavering support and expertise, this endeavor would not have been possible. The following individuals and organisations have played a significant role in shaping and propelling this venture, and for that, I am truly grateful.

Leading the way is Google, whose Language Facilitator has been instrumental in introducing Urdu to a wider audience. With its sophisticated algorithms, Google has paved the way for Urdu poetry to flow effortlessly through these pages. I have taken the help of *rekhta.org* as well and I wish to thank them.

I must acknowledge NuVoice Press, a creative hub that has provided me with a platform for innovative ideas and expressions.

Kevin Missal, the visionary leader at the helm of NuVoice, has been a constant source of inspiration throughout this journey. A special mention goes out to their dedicated editorial team, led by Ms. Navya Singh, whose diligence and expertise have refined the manuscript and turned words into a poetic work of art. Finally, their innovative design and production team deserves a round of applause for working round the clock to get the lovely book baby out.

Attention all marketing geniuses at HubHawks, your strategic brilliance was instrumental in gaining the attention of eager readers for this project, so please accept my heartfelt thanks for the same.

A round of applause to the meticulous distribution team at Simon & Schuster, whose efforts paved the way for these words to reach readers far and wide across the globe.

To my family, the unsung heroes who have stood by me throughout this journey, your unwavering support and understanding have made this experience not only possible but also extraordinary.

To the passionate septuagenarians and octogenarians, who recounted to me those dark days and helped me embark on this literary voyage, you represent the heartbeat of these tales. Thank you for breathing life into these words. To me, you are the friends of my father, and you are special.

About the Author

Kumar Kinshuk is an alumnus of T.A. Pai Management Institute (TAPMI), Manipal. He is a Gold Medalist graduate from St. Xavier's College, Ranchi University, and he did his schooling at St. Anthony's School, Ranchi.

He has worked in multiple industries over the last two decades and has been a keen marketer and an avid salesperson. He is a Co-Founder & Designated Partner in a newly launched real estate development enterprise.

Kinshuk has written five novels and a compendium of short stories. He has recently published a novel, "Darling, You're Obsessed" which is a blend of YA romance with the suspense thriller genre. Prior to that, he published an entire series called "The Kanke Killings". It is a compendium of four novels in the Police Procedurals genre. One of them, the "Ritualistic Murder" is a Thriller, while the other three novels, "Two Indian Girls", "Fatal Belief", and "Daybreak" are Mysteries. He has also published a novella, "Bariatu Tales" wherein he has dealt with the playful times of yore. It is a children's book that the adults of the 1960s and 70s would enjoy.

Kinshuk dabbles in photography and Nazms (Urdu Poetry) in his free time. He simply adores his kitchen garden and loves making various kinds of salads from home-grown items like lettuce, Italian basil etc. He lives in Kolkata with his better half, Sony and his daughter, Aryahi. His son, Aryan, works in Bengaluru.

Kinshuk loves spending time with his family and friends, and he takes part in community celebrations with gusto.